Chester Gore Miller

Father Junipero Serra

A new and original historical drama in four acts

Chester Gore Miller

Father Junipero Serra
A new and original historical drama in four acts

ISBN/EAN: 9783337105730

Printed in Europe, USA, Canada, Australia, Japan

Cover: Foto ©Andreas Hilbeck / pixelio.de

More available books at **www.hansebooks.com**

Father Junipero Serra,

A NEW AND ORIGINAL HISTORICAL DRAMA, IN FOUR ACTS.

BY

CHESTER GORE MILLER.

(DRAMATIC WORK, THE SECOND.)

ILLUSTRATED.

CHICAGO:

PRESS OF SKEEN, BAKER & CO.

1894.

CONTENTS.

FATHER JUNIPERO SERRA

PREFACE.

In California, August 28, 1884, services were held to commemorate the one hundredth anniversary of the death of Padre Junipero Serra; and the memorable occasion gave to the author at that time the idea of writing an historical-pastoral drama on the life of the saintly man so identified with the early annals of the state. The play was written in Chicago, in 1890, '91, '92, and '93.

While the Franciscan Friars who brought the light of Christianity to the shores of California were educating her savages, and founding her historical monuments, there grew up in purity and simplicity a matchless existence, referred to as "The Old Mission Days;" the most beautiful picture of pastoral life the world has ever known; now chronicled by a record, a ruin, and a memory. But though unfortunately that time is past, it served to show the worthy influence of the first pioneers, and particularly of their leader, a man whose name shall ever shine pre-eminent in the history of the Western Coast,—The Very Reverend Father Junipero Serra.

C. G. MILLER.

CHICAGO, ILL., Oct. 1893.

José the vacquero told her of
 some rare ferns & wild flowers

DEDICATION.

O California, an empire's star,
Upon your beauty time has made no raid;
Along your shores one finds no flaw to mar
The fairest work that Nature ever made.
Had I the gift to write a sonnet sweet,
To dedicate a eulogy to you,
My fourteen lines I fear would scarcely meet
The right inscription that I know is due.
For eighteen years within your border-lines
Showed me some prototypes I would not wrong:
Romantic land, the riches of your mines
O'er-shadow not your poetry and song.
    My recollections I would ne'er dismiss;
    In mem'ry then of you inscribed is this.

SAN CARLOS DEL CARMELO. DEDICATED, SEPTEMBER, 1797.

PROLOGUE.

Those who attend immunity from care,
Should on the Mission Fathers' lives reflect;
They, subjects of a fleeting time's impair,
Left lessons which too many oft neglect.
Along the coast and on the desert waste
They toiled, with true religious zeal their thought;
For martyr here and there a cross was placed,
Those deaths they envied, those the crowns they sought.
None asked their help and found that help refused;
His race, his caste, his creed, barred not their door,
The path to which the rich and humble used,
Some sorrow to relieve, some hope restore.
    Few lives can show a more exalted state;
    Their virtues no brief proem can relate.

DRAMATIS PERSONÆ.

Very Rev. Junipero Serra, president of the Missions.
Rev. Francisco Palou, of Mission San Francisco.
Rev. Matias Noriega, of Mission San Carlos.
Eduardo Ortega, a protegé of Father Serra.
Ignacio, a neophyte.
Don Pedro Fages, governor of California.
Captain Manuel Alvarez, of the governor's staff.
Don Pablo Valencia, a ranchero.
Doña Dolores, his daughter
Doña Eulalia, wife of Governor Fages.
Doña Barbara, a duenna.
     Neophytes.

ACT I.

HOME OF THE GOVERNOR. MONTEREY, CAL. THE
GARDEN, AFTERNOON, MARCH 18, 1784.

Enter Gov. Fages and Manuel.

Gov. Fages. Where seems the least oft 'times exists
the most.

Manuel. What! do you mean that he admires her?

Gov. Fages. · Yes.

Manuel. I thought that holy orders— .•

Gov. Fages. Well, you know
He 's not a novice yet, and so they see 𝟏
Each other often; now let friendliness
Grow into love—I 'm almost sure it has—
Then he 'll renounce all hopes of monkish life:
Dolores holds him high in her regard,
Yes more than any one in Monterey.
His mystic vein is his advertisement.

Manuel. What makes you think this love is possible?

Gov. Fages. I judge by way he looks at her.

Manuel. He looks!
Would that not be a trifling evidence?

Gov. Fages. If so I should not count it such a fact.

Manuel. Eduardo, my old friend so dear to me,
Had oft in early boyhood days remarked
Of pious ways, appearing as inclined
To serve the Church, as I to serve the State:

I know he is a youth of powerful will,
And when he once determines on a course
There 's nothing that would turn him from his path.

    Gov. Fages. Man's love is ever stronger than his will;
So fear the competition for her hand.

    Manuel. I do not care! I 'll risk the rivalry!
The conquest I expect an easy one;
She kissed the rose I gave her, murmuring
So gently, a sweet, *"Gracias,* Señor."

    Gov. Fages. I hope you 'll find the task an easy one.

    Manuel. Ah, Governor, but she is beautiful.
She 's not a type, she is a poet's dream;
I never saw such matchless grace before.

    Gov. Fages. Now, Manuel, just reason on this plan.
You want Dolores for your wife, and by
Your perseverance and my influence
You win, and wealth 's a certainty; through you
Her father 'll be in sympathy with me,
Thereby, my rule of state is doubly strong,
And Padre Serra's rising power is checked;
Don Pablo's influence at Court is great,
He 's hardly on my side.   Ah, *como no?*
Some viceroys come from humble walks in life,
Some from the velvet paths hidalgos tread;
And those sustained by seconds at the call
Obtain the recognition of the king.
We 've always worked for common interests
Since you came out from Spain two years ago,
And as your father was my warmest friend
You got a first lieutenancy to start,
And now you are a captain.

Manuel.   Thanks to you.
We are ambitious and our chance is good.

Gov. Fages.   Let your ambition unpretending be
Or else mistrust of motive will result.
Great possibilities are offered us,
The more advanced, the safer we become:
Our occupation 's kindred, that of arms,
But nerve 's demanded if we wish to rise;
Ah! I was taught that in Chihuahua once.
It 's only influence that keeps us here
And helps us to advance to higher planes;
So when opponents cry, "You grasping thieves,"
In jealousy because they do not rise,
We 've but to answer back with louder cry,
"See what we 've done in our short term of power,
Assail us not for we are virtuous."

Manuel.   I 'm with the moving spirit of the State,
So do not fear for my diplomacy.

Gov. Fages.   Just so, you 're apt and understand the
       scheme;
It takes the State to grind the Clergy down.
Talk to your friend and urge him for the Church,
For I believe myself it 's best for him;
In course of love, a friendship must not stand.
Now here he comes.

Manuel.   We only need to speak
Of absent ones to call their presence forth.

    Enter Eduardo.   *Walks to Crucifix on Wall.*

    Eduardo.   Age me on, O Years, age me on; but may
wisdom keep an equal pace; if not, let youth and its follies bloom on forever.

Enter Father Serra.

Gov. Fages. He bears with evident pride the antici-
pation of his calling.

Father Serra. Yes, but with a spiritual pride, not
worldly.

Gov. Fages. A gifted youth I'm told,—he should be
proud.

Father Serra. The man fortunate in natural gifts has
not the right or reason to be proud; they are posses-
sions no work of his attained.

Manuel greets Eduardo aside.

Gov. Fages. Don Pablo will be here.

Father Serra. I shall be glad to see him.

Gov. Fages. What of the converts? Have your efforts
increased the number of catechumens? I hear those
strange Indians from the interior are very wild.

Father Serra. So far I have been unsuccessful; they
are haughty and insolent; the protection is inadequate.
It will be some time before they acknowledge the Papal
jurisdiction.

Gov. Fages. The State.

Father Serra. Pardon me, the Church.

Gov. Fages. I can spare no more soldiers at present.

Father Serra. But San Carlos is in constant danger,
it is the same at all the Missions. I received a letter
from Father Figuer, saying, that San Diego just es-
caped another massacre through the piety of a neophyte;
and at San Buenaventura, Fathers Dumetz and Santa
Maria are having trouble with the natives. Do you wish

my flock to share the fate of Father Jaume, the martyr of our cause?

Gov. Fages. I do not wish them massacred; you are but two leagues from Monterey.

Father Serra. And after the pagans have attacked us, you desire to be notified? .

Gov. Fages. There is really little to dread; do not be afraid.

Father Serra. Dread! Fear! Too often have I longed to be a martyr for our Faith, that happiness has been withheld. I do not fear the savage or his knife; his anger or his treachery; it is for the innocents within my charge I am alarmed and would stay the march of rapine, murder, and of fire.

Gov. Fages. My army is very small.

Father Serra. You must request more men of the viceroy or we shall never carry out the grand idea of civilizing these savages.

Gov. Fages. Stay your enthusiasm, take time, all these things will be accomplished in time.

Father Serra. Governor, nothing is won by procrastination. I cannot consent to waste or wait one hour in this great work, and see these vast opportunities remain undeveloped. Why are we here? to idly dream away the hours and let the spirit of conversion die? see these countless ones born and grow up without the baptismal Sacrament? sin without the purification of the Sacrament? marry without the Sacrament? die without the Sacrament? He commands the Fathers spread the blessed Faith; I am His humble servant, and in my poor efforts His wishes shall not receive neglect, or His holy work want for activity.

Gov. Fages.   Step into my study, I've documents for you to sign, and letters for you from Los Angeles.

Father Serra.   There are other things I also wish to speak about, Governor. Eduardo, did you have Vicente notify the Indians of the rancheria, that we would begin the cultivation of their tract on a more extensive scale the coming week?

Eduardo.   Yes, Father.

Father Serra.   The move is wise. The land will soon supply their wants more generously.

Exeunt Father Serra and Gov. Fages.

Eduardo.   How poor the mail facilities have been.

Manuel.   Yes, when one's on an Indian campaign His correspondence must be limited.

Eduardo.   What have you heard from Spain?

Manuel.   There's nothing new;
My mother's well but father feels his age.
You got my letter saying Agata
Was married?

Eduardo.   Yes, she wedded very well.

Manuel.   I've only one unmarried sister left.

Eduardo.   Yes, so you have. Well, you have risen fast;
I am so glad to hear of your success:
I feel it's not to be a distant day
When it will please his majesty, our king,
To place you here high in authority.

Manuel.   Ah, should it be thus ordered so, that you
Are president and I executive,

I know that we will never differ on
These much vexed questions of the Church and State.
   Eduardo.   There, Manuel, is all this not a shame?
What storms at times beat round the Holy Cross.
Our noble, wise, far-seeing president,
Who 's most enthused to spread abroad the light
And found more mission churches on the coast,
Is constantly kept back for want of help;
Don Pedro should co-operate with us,
Instead of that his Excellency hopes
Forever to destroy or maim the rules
And system that have built the Missions up,
And make the Clergy ask of him their laws
In California.   Can you tell me
Who pioneers the way to lands unknown,
And plants the seed of civilized control?
Who sends abroad those men that oft become
The martyrs for the cause of holy truths?
Who struggles with the Indian, to give
His soul the blessings of a nobler faith?
Who ever thrives through grace of tenets true,
In places where all others failure meet?
And who a universal love commands,
Won by its purpose, system and its creed?
To all these questions there 's but one response:
The Church of Rome!
   Manuel.   All that you say is true;
And I regret Fages is so opposed.
   Eduardo. You have his confidence, you 'll help us some?
   Manuel. I 'll push my aid to the extent allowed,
But in my office I must be discreet.

Eduardo. I know discretion must remain your rule,
And though I ask you to assist our plans,
Do not do so and be unjust to him;
The Church gains not its rights dishonestly.
Ah, Manuel, I love this savage land,
There is so much to do; look o'er the miles
Of mountain chain, and vale, and endless plain,
Which virgin ground no white has ever trod:
Think of the countless souls to be redeemed;
What noble opportunities for us
In the near future of this western world.

Manuel. The vista is a most attractive one.
How proud I 'd be to know that you were called
'His Eminence, the Cardinal;' strive on!

Eduardo. There, do not speculate upon my end,
For where is my beginning?

Manuel.   You are right,
Because the more one dwells on sentiment
The harder do the trials of life appear.

Eduardo. If supposition were to us the truth,
What unsubstantial things would rule the world.

Manuel. Your life, I judge must be a peaceful one.

Eduardo. My life 's a quiet one and glides along
In channels of obscurity and peace;
Devoid of common stormy incidents,
Its elements would tiresome annals make:
I study, meditate, and help to keep
The Mission books, and as we 're short of help,
I 'm secretary to his Reverence.

Manuel. A restful life, I 've often longed for that;
I weary sometimes of the stormy life

The soldier of the line must undergo:
I most prefer the station I now hold,
That 's garrisoned within the capital.
But of your future, have you that defined?

  Eduardo. My future is unquestioned by myself;
The coming year a novice I shall be·
In San Fernando College, Mexico.
Our Padre Serra is to me a guide;
He took compassion on my lonely life,
When father died.

  Manuel. Now quite two years ago.
How time retreats.

  Eduardo. Yes, then he said to me,
"Eduardo, you are now alone, you have
No brothers, sisters, or near relatives;
Come live with me, I 'll be your counselor."

  Manuel. You 're fortunate in having such a man
To help you through these years.

  Eduardo. Indeed I am,
I 'm doubly fortunate, for I have you;
Your friendship and regard to me is much.

  Manuel. Eduardo, friend, I feel the same toward you,
I know it is returned.

  Eduardo. Yes, Manuel,
It is returned, and may it ever be.

  Manuel. What of the fair Dolores, that I 've met?
She came from Barcelona?

  Eduardo. No, you heard
No doubt our native town was once her home.
The don came from Madrid to Monterey
Just after you had left us for the South,

To join Don Pedro, which was—let me think—
    Manuel.   The month succeeding our arrival here.
    Eduardo.   O, yes.
    Manuel.   His daughter is a charming girl.
    Eduardo.   Dolores is a good girl and devout.
I 've known her from the time she first arrived.
    Manuel.   I came two days ago, I met her then.
    Eduardo.   Her mother has been dead some seven years.
    Manuel.   Eduardo, did you ever love?
    Eduardo.   Love? Yes,
Indeed I have.
    Manuel. Aside. The governor was right. *To Eduardo.*
So you have loved. Whom do you love, old friend?
    Eduardo.   Whom, Manuel? I love the Lord above,
I love the Fathers that teach us His words, —
    Manuel.   A noble answer, friend. You never loved
A woman?
    Eduardo.   Yes, my mother, Manuel.
    Manuel.   A proper adoration. *Aside.* Wrong; Fages.
-I 'll have no rival for her hand in him.
    Eduardo.   O, while it is in mind, his Reverence
Wished me to see the adjutant upon
A matter, so I 'll leave you for awhile.
    Manuel.   All right, Eduardo, I 'll see you again.

              Exit Eduardo.

The sun appears escorted by the moon,
To look is to be lost, I would be lost.
Depart my heart. How graceful she does move.

Enter Doñas Dolores and Barbara. Do not see Manuel.

Dolores. That is appropriate, Barbara; I am often in those moods. I sometimes think I will live and die unloved.

Manuel. Aside. Not while I am in Monterey.

Doña Barbara. Surely, Dolores, you have no occasion to think that.

Manuel. Aside. Not in the least.

Dolores. I know, I know; I have many friends among the gentlemen.

Manuel. Aside. Rivals!

Dolores. They are all liked by me—

Manuel. Aside. All!

Dolores. But no one do I feel I love.

Manuel. Aside. Then I do not inspire love on sight. I often wondered if I did.

Dolores. And were I forced to choose I could blindly pick one from the lot and have no fear of making a mistake.

Manuel. Aside. What an interesting lot of men in Monterey.

Doña Barbara. You will not waver when you meet your fate.

Manuel. Aside. If that's the case, my cause is lost.

Dolores. Possibly, and yet my love may be of the progressive kind.

Manuel. Aside. A chance remains!

Dolores. Not of the love on sight, nor yet the kind where one must learn to love.

Manuel. Aside. What variety the passion has!

Doña Barbara. What is the other kind?

Dolores. That sweet unconsciousness of it that ripens

into love on long acquaintance, it is the best and lasts the longest.

Manuel. Aside. I wish I had met her about ten years ago.

Doña Barbara. The lottery when tried will tell.

Manuel. Aside. How very wise she is.

Dolores. Do not speak as if love was an art to be experimented with. I shall never love but once, and when I do, it will be love.

Manuel. Aside. O Fortune, smile on me.

Doña Barbara. Coming. in? Señora Fages wishes you to sing for her this afternoon.

Dolores. I will be in soon.

Doña Barbara. Very well.   *Exit.*

Dolores plays Guitar and sings.

What more allays love's groundless fears,
When from the shadowed eve in song
Breaks softly sweet on list'ning ears,
The vows for which fond lovers long.

There hidden by day's curtain, night,
In low andante speaks the fate
That leads two souls from dark to light,
What happiness those chords create.

For 'neath some ancient cypress limb
He stands, and sings of constant ties;
Of love I 'd dream till stars grow dim
And stately night for morning dies.

Love's charm enhances every bar,
These happy hours too swiftly run;
Fain would I hear that sweet guitar
Till ' Good night' greets the morning sun.

When Time's light footfalls die away
And parting youth its age has hailed,
Of such sweet eves that close the day,
Say not of me, ' Remembrance failed.'

Manuel. "Say not of me, 'Remembrance failed.'"

Dolores. Why, Don Manuel! how you startled me.

Manuel. Forgive your willing slave.

Dolores. This time, but I would call you friend.

Manuel. You favor me, though he who is your friend would be your slave.

Dolores. As you select, Señor. But what was it you first remarked?

Manuel. "Say not of me, 'Remembrance failed.'"

Dolores. Of what?

Manuel. Two things.

Dolores. The first?

Manuel. The longing that the song expressed. I shall remember that you love the serenade.

Dolores. I do.

Manuel. Expect me then.

Dolores. I shall be pleased to hear you sing. And now the other?

Manuel. I would remember a sweet example of the only joy in life.

Dolores. And only one? There are many I am sure.

Manuel.   There is but one.

Dolores.   I should like to know of it.

Manuel.   A woman's voice.

Dolores.   What makes you think so?

Manuel.   I heard you sing.

Dolores.   Now, Señor, my voice would hardly cause—

Manuel.   Perfection needs no apology.

Dolores.   Indeed!   Have I attained that coveted end?

Manuel.   In every grace composing woman's charms.

Dolores.   Captain, will you receive advice?

Manuel.   You would honor me to give it.

Dolores.   Then go to court immediately.

Manuel.   Why, Señorita?

Dolores.   Though hardly an adept in the art of flattery, in fact I believe this is a first attempt, still you show great promise, it would make your fortune in time.

Manuel.   I would go—but for one thing.

Dolores.   And what is that?

Manuel.   I should have to leave good company

Dolores.   You would find better.

Manuel.   Impossible, for from perfection there is no appeal.

Dolores.   You are improving.

Manuel.   Why not, I have a teacher mistress of the art.

Dolores.   The pupil is an able one.

Manuel.   In errors and in faults.

Dolores.   You desire to excel?

Manuel.   That I may pay you graceful compliments.

Dolores.   Then remember subtilty is the character of flattery; for lavish praise incites suspicions of insincerity. .

Manuel. Did my well-deserved and well-intentioned compliments seem insincere?

Dolores. I imagine so, Señor.

Manuel. They were true expressions of my heart, and I am sure you will accept them for their worth. Woman and flattery are not antagonists.

Dolores. I fear your proverb is at fault.

Manuel. How so?

Dolores. Give the all-sweeping proverb an occasional exception.

Manuel. I see it needs a saving clause.

Dolores. Is your taste an admired one?

Manuel. My comrades call me, "Judge."

Dolores. Then, Judge, you have been bribed.

Manuel. In what way?

Dolores. To tell me what you have.

Manuel. You are right, I have been bribed.

Dolores. Now confess your object. Was it not to gain my regard?

Manuel. Though I would cherish that as the priceless treasure of my life; it was your beauty that urged me to flattery.

Dolores. And my perfections?

Manuel. Caused me to make my praise so forcible.

Dolores. I wonder if my father or Barbara think as you?

Manuel. Our relatives will ever find a fault.

Dolores. Some flatter by a smile, a look, a word, for—

Manuel. I need a phrase!

Dolores. Don Miguel once said I had a pretty hand;

Don Juan remarked of sparkling eyes; Señor Pacheco ventured comment on a little foot; and others beauty-praising bent, have smiled a favor, glanced a tribute, or risked a modest compliment; and I believed their offerings: but—

Manuel. They had poor taste if they could say no more.

Dolores. But you go to extremes, and say each grace is perfect in itself.

Manuel. Am I not right?

Dolores. Far from being so.

Manuel. You do not see what others note.

Dolores. The mirror tells me all.

Manuel. And does it not reflect perfection when you look?

Dolores. No.

Manuel. Discard the glass, its faults are serious.

Dolores. The Señora Gobernadora is calling us.

Manuel. We must obey.

Dolores. Do you remain for any length of time in Monterey?

Manuel. If I had to wish the time, I'd say for life, but being at the king's command, I will say it is indefinite. I can only hope that there will be many such days as this, in store for me.

Dolores. This afternoon is worthy of the morn, for that was matchless too.

Manuel. I was not referring to the day, Señorita.

Dolores. Your companion?

Manuel. My companion.

Dolores. So you like Monterey.

Manuel. Although it is a charming place, I love her
people more.

Dolores. The ladies in particular?

Manuel. A lady in particular. *Exeunt.*

Enter Father Serra and Don Pablo.

Don Pablo. I 've noticed that this Captain Alvarez
Is paying marked attention to my child,
Although it 's but the second time they 've met.
About his family I am informed,·
He 's from a noble line—important fact.
But then our growing youth of gentle blood
Have not the isolation found at home,
So of his habits and his character
I 'd like to know; perhaps your Reverence
Has knowledge of his ways?

Father Serra. Wise query, sir.
Though confidant to our opponent, yet
I cannot other then speak well of him.
A soldier, still he 's not a brawling one
So far as I have seen or heard report.
And then he seems as virtuous to-day
As when I knew him some two years ago:
He is Eduardo's friend—that favors him.
Yet it is with regret I have observed
That smiling innocence of face and ways
Announce not always innocence of heart;
He 's with a man who 'll stoop to any means
To gain an end,—environment you know
Has much to do with moulding character,—
Still he may be above that influence.

Don Pàblo.   He seems to be a most ambitious youth.
Father Serra.   But I am not one to call ambition,
          crime,
If one pursues an honest course to rise.
I think him worthy of your kind regard.
   Don Pablo.   I thank you, Father, now I 'll rest at ease.

"Above and from the south there came a sight
Wild geese that northward flew in rows of might
Till in the misty air float their traces——

Enter Eduardo.

Don Pablo.   No doubt, Eduardo, you are glad to meet
Your friend again?
   Eduardo.   Indeed I am, Señor.
   Father Serra.   And he is glad to be in Monterey?

Eduardo. He loves the capital, your Reverence;
But at San Carlos he would ever dwell.
Don Pablo. Few can resist the fascination there,
And as for me I 'm anything but proof.
How wise has been your choice of mission sites;
San Carlos ever will attract the eye.
One pleasure of my life is to observe
The sunrise o'er the distant Gabilans.

    This early morn I gazed on Nature's face,
        Around me in a dim and hazy light
        Lay Mission fields; adjoining on my right,
    Built by the sons of a converted race,
    San Carlos loomed in all its hallowed grace.
        Above and from the south there came in sight,
        Wild geese that northward flew in noisy flight,
    Till in the misty air I lost their trace.
    To hear the Padre read an early Mass,
        The Indians came, and blest, then bending low
    They prayed; the service o'er, I saw them pass
        To labor, walking single file and slow:
    The mist had gone, like breath upon a glass,
        For o'er the range appeared a crimson glow.

Father Serra.   How constantly I 've wished, and
      worked, and prayed,
To see such early-morn devotionals
In every vale of California.
But nine far-scattered missionary posts
Through which the great Redeemer has to speak,
Are the results of fifteen years of work.

Don Pablo.   Does not your Reverence expect to found
A line of missions to the east of us?

Father Serra.   I have expected to for many years.

Don Pablo.   I 'm sure San Juan Bautista, San José,
Most holy San Miguel, and San Raphael,
Would kindly smile on California,
Were missions titled with their holy names.

Father Serra.   Ah, not alone the blessed saints re-
    marked,
But others of the Faith:—the Mystery,
La Purísima de Concepcion,
Then Santa Cruz, and Santa Barbara,
Nuestra Señora de la Soledad,
Santa Ynéz, San Francisco Solano,
There 's San Fernando and San Louis Rey,
Aye, San Antonio de Pala—all—
Should,—shall have missions dedicated them!

Don Pablo.   What causes this delay, your Reverence?

Father Serra.   We came to Alta California,
With promise from the State to found, equip,
And guard for us, new missions by the score;
Now that the country has been settled up
So to withstand the Russians southward march;
The State relapses into lethargy,
Forgetful of its pledge.

Don Pablo.   So that is what
Retards the propagation of the Faith?

Father Serra.   Just so. None but Neglect's regardless
    eye
Observes these countless opportunities:
So I must fight inaction coupled to

The opposition of a governor,
Whose policy is secular control.
  Don Pablo. A state of things that 's most deplorable.
  Father Serra. Don Pablo, it has been a fear with me,
That when the Padre pioneers would die
Or age retire them to Mexico;
Would pass away the vigor to resist
Encroachments and delinquencies of state:
But here is one in whom I 've centered hopes;
For when Eduardo is ordained, he 'll push
With all the zeal of youthful energy,
The spirit of our views.
  Eduardo.   I know them well;
And this shall be the mission of my life.
  Don Pablo. A future 's opened to the faithful priest
In these extensive wilds. You feel assured
You would succeed in churchly work?
  Eduardo.   I do.
Oft have I felt within, the call Divine.
I 'll not be tempted to forego my choice.
  Father Serra. Quite right, one must believe they 're
    called to serve.
  Eduardo. May duty ever be allied to me,
As cross to pyx; or chausable to stole.
  Father Serra. It 's duty to the laws Divine that move
These countless spheres within that waste of space;
And as His works inanimate obey,
Then so should they, with His fair form endowed,
Be not delinquent to the given Word.

            Enter Gov. Fages.

Father Serra.   Governor, is Lieutenant Gonzales here to-day?

Gov. Fages.   I left him within.

Father Serra.   *To Eduardo.*   You saw the adjutant?

Eduardo.   Yes, Father, I have the data you require.

Father Serra.   I must see the lieutenant, gentlemen. Come, son.   *Exeunt.*

Don Pablo.   A bright and pious youth, the Father's protege.

Gov. Fages.   It seems the thoughtful lean to religion.

Don Pablo.   Governor, I have decided at last to remain in California.

Gov. Fages.   Indeed!   I am glad to hear this.

Don Pablo.   I understand California is becoming favorably known among the caballeros of old Spain.

Gov. Fages.   Very good, we shall not lack for society. Your family like the West?

Don Pablo.   They beg me to remain.

Gov. Fages.   A weighty inducement.

Don Pablo.   Besides, my health, for which I came, you know, has greatly improved.

Gov. Fages.   That is all the more reason you should stay with us.   But you will make a final visit to Madrid?

Don Pablo.   To settle my affairs, and pay a parting mark of homage to his majesty.

Gov. Fages.   *Aside.*   And whisper praises of a most devoted governor.   *To Don Pablo.*   When do you expect to make the journey?

Don Pablo.   The coming year.

Gov. Fages.   In what will you engage now you 're to be a Californian?

Don Pablo.. My regular pursuit, cattle raising; which
I hope to undertake on a more extensive scale. So, Don
Pedro, I am here to make request—

Gov. Fages. Name the tract. Señor, and it is yours.

Don Pablo. . The land on which the adjacent rancheria
stands.

Gov. Fages. *Aside.* Mission lands! *To Don Pablo.*
Shall be Valencia property.

Don Pablo. Thanks, Don Pedro, thanks. It is good
grazing ground.

Gov. Fages. Excellent. *Aside.* Serra spoke of cultivating a part of it, there must be no delay. *To Don
Pablo.* This property is beyond the four league limit of
Pueblo lands—somewhat out of my jurisdiction—a non-
important fact; for I shall recommend your petition to
the viceroy, and request the grant be made a regular
concession instead of provisional, as many now are made.

Don Pablo. You are very kind.

Gov. Fages. Don Manuel can make the papers out
to-night, and I can send them on the vessel that leaves
to-morrow for the South.

Don Pablo. I 'll hear from them before the summer 's
over?

Gov. Fages. Long before. Count on the land, you
will be granted it.

Don Pablo. I should like to inspect the tract more
fully than I have; could you spare an escort some day
the coming week? ·

Gov. Fages. My idle soldiers are impatient to respond.

Don Pablo. I am under heavy obligations to Don
Pedro.

Gov. Fages. I pray you make no mention of a bond.
Aside. One step nearer secularization; confusion to the president; the reciprocating friendship of Valencia: are gains that come upon me unannounced; so on its swift ascendant course my star of fortune brighter grows, as coming months bid parting ones farewell.

Enter Manuel.

Manuel. Don Pablo, our Señora Gobernadora was asking for you; she is telling the story of her journey across Mexico.

Don Pablo. By your leave, gentlemen, I will wait on the lady. *Exit.*

Manuel. Where seems the most oft' times exists the least.

Gov. Fages. What have you discovered?

Manuel. That Eduardo is in love.

Gov. Fages. So I said.

Manuel. With the Church.

Gov. Fages. I do not doubt it.

Manuel. But not Dolores.

Gov. Fages. How did you learn this?

Manuel. I questioned him.

Gov. Fages. Brilliant! Manuel, brilliant!

Manuel. Governor, for once you are deceived.

Gov. Fages. Are you aware a man can fall in love and not know it?

Manuel. Never heard of an instance.

Gov. Fages. I want you to dance the fandango with Dolores.

Manuel. A great pleasure.

Gov. Fages. Doña Eulalia will bring the dance about. I arranged it as an opening for you, and incidentally you may note the admiration I attribute to Eduardo.

Manuel. Many thanks, and I will watch him closely, provided that Dolores does not absorb my beauty-seeking gaze.

Gov. Fages. I have gained a point with Don Pablo.

Manuel. That is welcome. What is it?

Gov. Fages. He asked me for the San Carlos rancheria tract that Serra spoke about cultivating. The transport leaves to-morrow, and with it goes my recommendation that the land be granted him.

Manuel. Does Father Serra know of this?

Gov. Fages. No, and Valencia will not speak of it; he is very reticent about his private affairs.

Manuel. To grant this land will be quite in keeping with your secularization policy.

Gov. Fages. Certainly it will! Nothing will ruin the Missions like spoliation of their lands. Besides I could not be more fortunate, for can't you see, he will feel grateful for my help, and when I need a word at court he will respond;—you know Don Pablo's father once saved the king's life.

Manuel. No!

Gov. Fages. Yes, and that is why he stands so high at court.

Manuel. Well, this is fortunate!

Gov. Fages. As long as his Catholic Majesty does not look kindly on the friars' control of the temporalities, or anything else in fact, so much more fortunate for us; so when he sees I have worked for him he will reward.

Manuel. You are a diplomat.

Gov. Fages. Time will decide the value of my diplomacy.

Manuel. I hope we may succeed.

Gov. Fages. We shall succeed!

Manuel. My sword! my name! my honor! to the cause.

Gov. Fages. Win Dolores, that is the part you are to play.

Manuel. I understand Father Serra is here on official business.

Gov. Fages. Yes, I have seen him, but he desires to confer again; you may remain during the interview. I had better see him now.

Enter Eduardo.

Is Father Serra engaged?

Eduardo. I left his Reverence conversing with Captain Soler and Lieutenant Gonzales.

Enter Doñas Eulalia and Dolores.

Gov. Fages. Very well, we can see the Father later.

Doña Eulalia. Do we have music? Señorita Dolores will dance the cachucha.

Gov. Fages. You save me making the request; but let us have the fandango. Will Señorita dance with the captain?

Dolores. I should be pleased to, your Excellency.

Manuel. I am honored.

Enter Don Pablo.

Gov. Fages. Is Doña Barbara within? We are going to have a fandango.

Don Pablo. I will call her. *Exit.*

Doña Eulalia. What fine days you have in California.

Manuel. The climate is most attractive.

Dolores. So much like sunny Spain.

Doña Eulalia. I hear Father Serra contemplates another journey.

Eduardo. Yes, Señora, there are many confirmations to be made, and Santa Clara is to be dedicated in May.

Enter Doña Barbara and Don Pablo.

Gov. Fages. Señora, will you play a fandango for us?

Doña Barbara. With pleasure, your Excellency.

Gov. Fages. The fandango is my delight. It recalls the pleasures of my youth. *To Manuel.* Watch Eduardo and be convinced. *To Doña Barbara.* Ready, Señora.

Doña Barbara plays guitar, Manuel and Dolores dance. Eduardo watches Dolores with admiring gaze.
Dance over.

Doña Eulalia. They were very graceful.

Doña Barbara. They kept good time.

Gov. Fages. To one who played in perfect tune.

Doña Barbara. Thank you, Governor.

Enter Father Serra.

Doña Eulalia. How absorbed in thought Don Eduardo always seems, Father.

Father Serra. He is very thoughtful; better were all young men as serious. How is your son?

Doña Eulalia. Pedrito is now quite well; but, Father, you do not look to be in the best of health.

Father Serra. I shall not see the entry of the coming year.

Doña Eulalia. No, no, I cannot believe you are declining so.

Father Serra. It is that final failing from which there is no recovery.

Don Pablo. Señora, I am anxious to hear the rest of your narrative.

Doña Barbara. You stopped at a most interesting part.

Doña Eulalia. I am glad you liked it. Coming, Dolores? You were interested.

Dolores. Very much so.

Exeunt Doñas Eulalia and Barbara, and Don Pablo.

Manuel. This has been a great pleasure. I hope for a repetition.

Dolores. Señor is a charming dancer.

Manuel. A novice beside his partner.

Exit Dolores.

Gov. Fages. Aside to Manuel. Did you note your friend?

Manuel. Yes, but I think it is only admiration; none could help admiring her.

Gov. Fages. You will yet be convinced.

Father Serra. Aside to Eduardo. My son, is my com-

munication to the viceroy complete, so that I can forward
it to-morrow if the governor refuses my request?

Eduardo.   Yes, Father, I wrote in the information I'
obtained from the adjutant-inspector, so all wanting is
your signature.   Will you sign?

Father Serra. Keep it, son, I do not need it yet. Now,
Governor, have you leisure?

Gov. Fages.   I am at your service.   *To Manuel.* You
are the audience, so be amused.

Father Serra.   What I 'm to say will take but little
         time;
In substance it 's the same as you have heard:
The first and most important point of all—
This very pressing want of Mission guards.
I ask again, consider this request;
The men we have are poor apologies:
It seems we always have the poorest drilled.
Conversion is retarded by this want
Of adequate protection to our homes.

Gov. Fages.   Give you more soldiers, that I cannot
         do:
I wish you 'd let this tiresome subject drop.

Father Serra.   Will you detail some men to follow up
The neophytes, and bring them back to us?

Gov. Fages.   I have no men to hunt apostates now.

· *Father Serra.*   Desertion is a serious offence;
You let them go, and so encourage it.

Gov. Fages.   I do not make your converts, renegades.

Father Serra.   You do not advocate the fault direct,
But tolerate the wrong, which is as bad.

Gov. Fages.   You take entirely too much care of them;

They would improve and do as well beneath
The military law and State's decree.
    Father Serra.   The State would educate but never
        does,
Its education lacks religious thought,
So teaches to the youthful mind in vain.
No one is learned, knowing naught of Faith;
Let Indians grow committed to the State's
Paternal care, and there will issue forth
A class of beings ignorant and poor;
Conditioned lower than they were by birth:
And in the place of peace and Christian life,
God-fearing natives, virtuous and good;
There is the bowl, the riot of the camp,
While flaunting sin its late hour revels keep:
Then comes a fast disintegration, and
From customed union do they drift away
As seeds are swept by trades to other climes;
The wreckage of a race that then remains,
Must see extinction overcome their tribe.
    Gov. Fages.   How dismal do you make their future
        out.
I cannot help you now—I may next year.
The more that leave the less there are to feed.
They 'll all return in time, so let them go.
    Father Serra.   Never! can I consent to lose one soul,
That by salvation would that soul reclaim!
'T would be a crime for us to disregard
Such heavy loss brought on through negligence:
To see one poor misguided Indian
Return to those unfathomed darkened depths

From whence his soul emerged. It must not be!

Gov. Fages. Though souls be lost or saved, I 've not
    the men;

I need the few I have for other things.

Aside. If nothing else, to drill within the fort. *To
Father Serra.* Pass to the next request.

Aside. And be refused.

Father Serra. Will you equip a party to select

The mission sites for the interior?

Gov. Fages. For this great scheme I 'm also unpre-
    pared.

Father Serra. Well, what of the new missions for
    the South;

La Purísima, Santa Barbara?

Are you prepared to have them founded now?

Gov. Fages. I shall postpone that work another
    year.

Father Serra. The Channel with its grand induce-
    ments must

Be then neglected for another year?

Gov. Fages. I gave my ruling on this old request.

Father Serra. How long do you allow the Church
    to live

In California?

Gov. Fages. The law forbids

My—

Father Serra. Not the law, you mean the governor:

The man who idles precious time away.

Gov. Fages. Aside. Ah, idle, am I? Well, not in a
    plot

That has your ruin for its pleasant aim. *To Father Serra.*

It is this never ending restless strife
To make conversion foremost in all moves,
That wearies me; I do not toil like you
And I will gain as much.

    Father Serra.   Without a doubt
You may accomplish all the ends you seek;
But I would shun the methods that you use.

    Gov. Fages.   My methods hardly seem in high repute
In California. That's bad for you:
The king, though, deems them ample for his needs.
You should forget there is a governor,
Then you would not be forced to make requests.

    Father Serra.   And these requests I make are but the
            rights
That have been granted us, and you withhold.
I 'd like oblivion upon the fact
That you must serve the king as governor:
Your office, like a number in the State,
Is far beyond the virtues of the man.

    Gov. Fages.   I 'm hearing this!

    Father Serra.   Well, I intend you shall:
For I would never say behind your back
What I would hesitate to speak to you.

    Gov. Fages.   Withhold your comments!—for I asked
            them not.

    Father Serra.   Like most officials you dislike the
            truth;
But those whom you would serve will welcome it.
I had you once removed—

    Gov. Fages.   You 'll not again!

    Father Serra.   For reservation of the friars' rights;

And had I now the health to journey south
And lay before the viceroy a report
Of how affairs are here administered;
You 'd not be governor another month.
But as it is I have a substitute.
The documents, Eduardo. Now, a pen.

Exit Eduardo.

Gov. Fages. Complain! complain! for I shall answer
you!
I have complaints about your ways as well.

ACT II.

SCENE I. Exterior of Don Pablo's Home. Afternoon, Late. June 3, 1784.

Enter Father Serra, Eduardo and Ignacio.

Father Serra. How very welcome is the half-way
    house.
I hope Don Pablo 's not away from home.
Announce we have arrived, Ignacio.
  Ignacio. Yes, Father.   *Exit.*
  Eduardo.   Do we stop here for the night,
Your Reverence?
  Father Serra.   Yes, for the hour is late:
San Carlos finds us home to-morrow noon.
  Eduardo. Aside. And I can look upon her face
again.

Enter Don Pablo and Ignacio.

  Don Pablo. Ah, Father, welcome; and Eduardo too.
Now I regret the pleasure I have missed,
To act your escort from the capital:
My willing horses ever wait your mount.
  Father Serra. You 're very kind, Don Pablo, but you
    know
The friars never ride. The road was good
Along the coast; all 's well at Monterey.
I missed the governor, they said he left

To visit you: I hope he still remains.
Don Pablo. The governor is here; he 'll stop three
    days;
He is attended by Don Manuel:
And the Señora also came with him.
    Father Serra. I shall be very glad to meet them all.
    Don Pablo. Now, Father, will you enter and take
    rest?
My house is yours.
    Father Serra. I do feel somewhat tired.
Eduardo, will you come?
    Eduardo. I would remain
Without, a little while, your Reverence.

    Exeunt Father Serra and Don Pablo.

Ignacio, whom did you see within?
    Ignacio. The governor and Captain Alvarez.
    Eduardo. I meant the ladies, did you see her there?
    Ignacio. You mean the Doña Bar—
    Eduardo. Dolores.
    Ignacio. Yes,—
    Eduardo. Now leave me for awhile, Ignacio.
    Ignacio. Joaquin the arriero is my friend;
Should I be needed I will be with him. *Exit.*
    Eduardo. For months the phantom of her lovely face
Has held a place beside my daily prayers:
I who have been so wedded to the Church.
How strange it seems. 'T was admiration first;
Then grew that longing for companionship:
The revelation followed on the day
I helped the Father don the alb; the act

Brought thoughts of my novitiate to come;
And then I found I could not say farewell;
I was in love,—how sweet the moment seemed:
It then occurred to me that I had sinned;
I prayed and in that prayer there came a thought,
'That pure and holy love was not a sin;
What He creates can never be a wrong.'
But when I laid that vestment in the chest,
It seemed I laid aside a noble work:
O, what a bitter argument commenced;
For one has but to choose of diverse paths,
To lay foundation for the mind's unrest.
It 's over now.   I 'll find her and confess.   *Exit.*

Enter Doñas Eulalia and Dolores.

Doña Eulalia.   I 'd favor him if I were you.
Dolores.   Why so?
Doña Eulalia.   Because he will be prominent in time.
Don Pedro favors him; when he does that
With one, his fortune is assured.
Dolores.   I hope
He 'll always be in favor then.
Doña Eulalia.   I think,
Dolores, you would like to see him rise.
Dolores.   No more than I would any one.
Doña Eulalia.   Who knows
But some day he might ask—
   Dolores.   ˙   Perchance— some day.

Enter Eduardo, crossing back of stage.

Eduardo.   She never is alone of late.   I'll write.
The pen is best, my courage might depart.   *Exit.*

Dolores. Now there is one who surely will be heard. .

Doña Eulalia. Yes, he is under the right tutelage.
Here 's one as worthy, and who is assured   .
Of honors from the State and from the king.

Enter Manuel.

Manuel. Well, ladies, *Á Dios.*

Dolores.   What, going now?

Manuel. Yes, still not far; I will be back at eve.

Doña Eulalia. But you must sing, you promised me
    you would.

Manuel. Official business.

Doña Eulalia.   Sing us just one song.

Manuel. Will not *mañana* do?

Doña Eulalia.   No, no, Señor.

Dolores. Here is the instrument, I 'm sure you will.

Doña Eulalia. I love to hear one sing that has a
    voice.

Manuel. I have a voice for calling orders out:
I also have a cold; I 'm always hoarse
When I am asked to sing. I better go
My two league trip, far up among the hills;
And when I 'm there in clearer atmosphere
I 'll sing to you a song of love or war,
Or, better still, of woman's constancy;
And let the distant echoes come to you
Well tempered and improved by passing winds.

Doña Eulalia. Now that excuse, Señor, will not avail:
As wife to your superior, I say,
Don Manuel, you must.

Dolores.   Hear that? Commence.

Manuel.   You know I have a grave suspicion that
My auditors will sadly slip away,
Before initial notes, crescendo, rise.
    Dolores.   That punishment is not in store for you.
    Doña Eulalia.   Your voice calls not for such severe
        neglect.
Sing of the sea.
    Dolores.   O yes, I love the see.

        Manuel plays guitar and sings.

O dwell 'mid the maritime pines;
   Go live near the sound of the sea;
On sands where the waves find their shrines;
   Let grief to forgetfulness flee.

Its wild stormy moods often seem
   Like times in one's life that are past:
Its calms, like the lulls which redeem,
   The life that misfortune would blast.

But sympathy sweet one can trace
   In waves which so ceaselessly roll:
The sad in the sea find a grace,
   And rest to the deep-burdened soul.

Yea, dream on the rocks of the shore;
   Heed not the rough blight of the years:
But let the great ocean restore
   Hopes lost in the past and in tears.

When pines to the sea sigh refrain;
   They speak to the wish that is dead:
The weary will find from the main;
   The light of good hope has not fled.

Dolores. The song was very sweet.
Doña Eulalia. Ah, *Capitan,*
I thought I heard you say you could not sing.

Enter Ignacio.

Ignacio. The governor would see Don Manuel. *Exit.*
Manuel. There, there, a reprimand; and you the
cause.
You kept me captive here.
Doña Eulalia. I 'll intercede.
Dolores. Tell him it was our fault.
Manuel. Of course it was.
Beware the wrath of the executive.
Doña Eulalia. We 're not afraid of him.
Dolores. Do tell him that.
I hope your ride will be a pleasant one.
Doña Eulalia. I 'm sure it will.
Manuel. Thanks. *A Dios,* again. *Exit.*
Dolores. Señora, you must see my garden now,
I have so many new varieties.
There is a lovely orchid from Peru,
That calls an Eastern Cordillera, home;
It 's named the Inca's Heart, white splashed with red.
My rarest orchid though, the gem of all,
Grew on a graven god of sacrifice
In mystic Yucatan. A friend of ours,
José Juares, sent the plants to us.
Doña Eulalia. Indeed, I wish to see them. Let us
go. *Exeunt.*

Enter Gov. Fages and Manuel.

Gov. Fages. On the road to the rancheria you pass San Carlos, avoid it.

Manuel. I shall. Well, *buenas tardes,* I may be back by Vespers.

Gov. Fages. Wait, there is no hurry; we have so little time together.

Manuel. Suppose I 'm going to be with you when we are at Rancho del Carrasco?

Gov. Fages. Bueno, bueno! Most important! How are your love affairs?

Manuel. Speak in the singular; I 've only one, I want no more. Over two months have passed and no encouragement.

Gov. Fages. Keep it up; make love to her at every opportunity; she will get tired and capitulate in time.

Manuel. That is not saying much for my attractions.

Gov. Fages. If one is not attractive, he must be attentive. You are attractive enough.

Manuel. What is it, then?

Gov. Fages. Never try to account for whims. Did the interpreter accompany us?

Manuel. Yes.

Gov. Fages. Be sure to take him along. You see how important it is to have a private understanding with the chief; Don Pablo, the other day, made mention of his need of more help, so I determined to supply the want.

Manuel. An excellent idea.

Gov. Fages. I had the sergeant bring an extra sword which you can present to the chief with some ceremony, —give him my regards and promise greater things to come.

Manuel. Very well. I might give him a pair of gloves I no longer use.

Gov. Fages. Contribute those when we have something else to ask of him. Obtain not less than ten runaway neophytes, and I think you had better let Sergeant Verdugo and four men take them first to Monterey, then they will appear as Presidio Indians.

Manuel. He will be pleased when he receives their services.

Gov. Fages. I am winning him step by step; why he said not an hour ago, I 'd make a splendid viceroy.

Manuel. He told the truth, but what occasioned it?

Gov. Fages. He is displeased with the way Matias de Galvez treated a friend of his who lives in Acapulco or Mazatlan, I have forgotten which.

Manuel. Of course you considered it a shame?

Gov. Fages. It was an outrage in my diplomatic eyes.

Manuel. And you sympathized?

Gov. Fages. He is the very picture of injured innocence that has been comforted. Mark me, before many months I will have him so bound by obligations, that when the king sends for reports of me, having in view an official change, Señor Valencia can inform his majesty, thus: "I am acquainted with the governor, an excellent executive."

Manuel. The king responds: "He 's an honor to the throne; promote Fages."

Gov. Fages. And Fages rules as commandant-general.

Manuel. To wait his turn as viceroy; while I—

Gov. Fages. March on at equal pace, though a little in the rear.

Manuel. To be viceroy when you enjoy the *residencia.*

Gov. Fages. Certainly! Everything is looking well for us. The Manila galleon will soon be here, and when she leaves for San Blas, she carries some new charges I am studying up regarding the friars' movements.

Manuel. Let no complaint stand unproclaimed. But their communication of last Spring may injure us.

Gov. Fages. I do not think so.

Enter Don Pablo.

Don Pablo. Well, gentlemen, I hope the hours pass pleasantly.

Gov. Fages. They do, Señor.

Manuel. You have the best located rancho in California, I like the name, Del Carrasco; it's so appropriate.

Gov. Fages. I always thought the southern half of this peninsula, with this magnificent view of Carmelo Bay and the Sierra Santa Lucias, was an ideal situation for a hacienda.

Don Pablo. The very reason I selected it. Señor Carrillo on his visit here, first brought it to my notice; and Señor Guerrero helped me stock the place.

Manuel. Did you not say, Don Pedro, that Señor Valencia's title to the ranchería tract would soon be up from Mexico?

Gov. Fages. Yes; it will be here the coming month.

Don Pablo. I feel under great obligations to you, Governor.

Gov. Fages. I 'm sure you will find the venture profitable.

Manuel. It is the finest property within a radius of twenty leagues.

Don Pablo. I thought the selection good. But what is to be done with the rancheria now upon it? That has worried me some of late.

Manuel. Move it off.

Don Pablo. The Fathers might object.

Gov. Fages. Charge the Indians rent.

Don Pablo. I 'll think it over.

Manuel. I will go, it is getting late.

Gov. Fages. Vamos!

Manuel. I have a mission to perform so I 'll be absent till Vespers.

Don Pablo. Wait, I will see you off. I 'll return directly, Governor.

Manuel. Á Dios.

Gov. Fages. Á Dios.

Exeunt Don Pablo and Manuel.

My enemy! I 'll smile on him to-day.

Enter Father Serra.

Father Serra. Now, Governor, returning to our wish;
To-day you were to give me your reply.
What do you say?

Gov. Fages. It must be, ' No,' again.

Father Serra. Are you to ever favor us?

Gov. Fages. As yet
I 've no authority to give you aid.

Father Serra.   This is within your power.

Gov. Fages.   Pardon me—

Father Serra.   How marvelous the office that you
hold!

Your power contracts and then expands at will;
When you could injure us, your sway is great;
When you could favor us, you 're limited.
But we will see what our complaints will bring.

Gov. Fages.   I hope the government will do for you.
I bend to hear the wishes of my king,
And when I know his wish I know my way:
The viceroy orders and to him I bow,
For is he not the king in Mexico?
I find the laws and they must be enforced:
He says your mail must not be carried free;
I think his regulation very wise:
So where am I to blame?

Father Serra.   No, sir, of late
He has not ordered so, we hear from him.
It has been understood a year or more,
The friars' letters should be carried free;
Based on the privilege I once obtained:
But you so far exceed the powers with which
You were invested by his majesty,
In your anxiety to injure us;
That regulations now long obsolete
Have been revived, and so enlarged upon
That they become the laws, administered
With due severity.

Gov. Fages.   How very strange
This great delusion, I your enemy.

I 'm your friend and better than you think.
   Father Serra.   What!
   Gov. Fages.   It 's a true assertion that I make;
Sometimes the actions of a friend appear
The actions of an enemy.
   Father Serra.   Stop, stop!
Don Pedro, stop! and speak no more like that:
You make yourself a glaring hypocrite.
A friend to us! O, what hypocrisy!
There 're times when friends seem to us enemies,
When striving to protect us from some harm;
But you are not that kind of friend to us.
   Gov. Fages.   I know the good you do, I am your
      friend;
I 'm always willing to concede, when the—
   Father Serra.   Of course, when the concession favors
      you.
I ask if you are well supplied with arms,
You answer, " Yes," and only wait the word
To be of use in crushing savage life;
Provided, that the venture gives to you
The reputation of a governor,
Whose conquests cast a glory on the throne:
But when I ask for peaceful means to tide
The flood of savagery around us here;
Those little things that help conversion much;
Those slight protections that would do no harm,
But awe the bold and reckless Indian;
You then become too helpless to assist,
And answer in that aggravating way,

Meant to divert the subject, or to tell
How much you love us for the good we do.
    Gov. Fages.   Now, now, when will these constant
        quarrels end?
    Father Serra.   When you have given to the Church
        its due.
Expecting peace, you aim your secret blows.
The lips, that utter overtures for peace
Designed in words as you presented now,
Profane the pax if thereon it were sealed.
The state affairs are rotten at the core
For lack of honest-hearted men to rule.
    Gov. Fages.   The state affairs as here administered—
Are just as pure as honesty can make.
    Father Serra.   Not in the least are our conclusions
        wrong;
These schemes of politics need strong reproof:
To gain ascendancy what ends some men
Will follow up in way of cunning arts;
Low subtle plans and dark intrigues for gain;
Duplicity renamed diplomacy;
Ends so contemptible they dare not let
The people know about; ends based upon
A motto that is secret to themselves;
Which were it blazoned forth the world would read,
"We live to grasp position, wealth and power;"
To which they add so but the conscience hears,
"The way that we ascend is shrouded black,
We 'll screen intentions by convenient laws,
In other words we 'll legalize a crime,
So silence, silence, silence is the word.

And then a guileless world will honor us,
And say of us, 'Gaze on those mighty men,
How well they earned the honors that we give;
How fortunate, what spotless lives they lead:' "
And in the consummation of this work
They do forget their fellows and their God,
And so the people have to bow beneath
The wisdom and dominion of the sword,
That 's wielded by an army picaroon.
Talk not to me of purity of state,
For such a strange condition never has
And never will exist, so long as man
Ignores the laws and teachings of the Church.

    Gov. Fages. Now, Father, will you ever be convinced
That you are wrong?

    Father Serra.   I 'll never be convinced.

    Gov. Fages. I 'll tell you what, here 's our respected
        friend;
But though he leans toward you in kindliness
More than to me, let him be judge of what
Is right upon this franking privilege;
I feel assured he will agree with me.

    Father Serra. Most willingly will I defer to him;
Though it 's mere pastime, still it will have weight:
I 'd like to have him know what we endure.

Enter Don Pablo.

Don Pablo, you have been appointed judge.

    Gov. Fages. Convince his Reverence that I am right.

    Don Pablo. Am at your service, Father, Governor.
What may the issue be? Come, go within,

And over some refreshment we 'll decide.

    Gov. Fages. Aside. By this I 'll see whom he will patronize:

If he appreciates what I have done

For him, my favors then will be his bribe.   *Exeunt.*

Enter Eduardo.

    Eduardo. Reading letter. "Señorita Dolores: Be my confessor now. That I love you do not misjudge as a sudden fancy, for the infatuation has with it the wealth of time. This is not in keeping with the course I intended to pursue, but on your word I will renounce the same to seek success in other than religious fields. If you refuse my poor oblation: return to me this writing on which you have indorsed the figure of the cross—if you accept, then write thereon your blessed name; so sacred to the Church, so hallowed in my heart. Dolores, decide the fate of Eduardo Ortega."

Always attended.

Enter Doñas Eulalia, Dolores and Barbara.

    Dolores. His Reverence is often met at prayer

Beneath those gnarled, grotesque and ghostly limbs.

    Doña Eulalia. At night, Dolores?

    Dolores.   Yes.

    Doña Eulalia.   O, holy man.

I sometimes marvel at his great success

In the conversion of the Indians:

I need not though with such devotion shown.

    Doña Barbara. To fail would be the marvel of his life.

Eduardo.   To pass him in his loftiness of thought,
Excel him in the greatness of his works,
Exceed him in his pious kindliness,
Transcend his deep devotion to our God,
Or still display more energy than he;
One could not do.
   Dolores.   You picture him in that.
   Doña Eulalia.   You came along the coast?
   Eduardo.   Yes, not around
Point Pinos, for that is too long a road.
The Father wished to gaze upon the sea
For southern sails, bound northward with supplies;

Although his watchfulness brought no reward.
Dolores. But then the way—what an unrivalled way
Eduardo. Ah, yes, indeed it is. This afternoon

The sun while sinking in the distant west,
    Was by the cumulus and stratus veiled;
    And in those vapor barriers prevailed
The wondrous tints, eve's hour makes manifest.
Outspreading like gigantic airy fans,
    The streaming rays through fleecy rifts to me
    Appeared, above the·still Pacific sea;
Reflecting golden shadows on the sands.
The scene, my mind so gently did enchain,
    That I sang out our Padre's evening psalm;
The Father joined me in the sweet refrain,
    And o'er my soul there came a rest so calm;
For in that song my feelings found release,
And life for once seemed one of perfect peace.

Doña Eulalia. What sweet content one draws from
    Nature's views.
Doña Barbara. Oft have I noticed such a scene as
    that
From our retreat.
Doña Eulalia. Where grow the cypress?
Doña Barbara. Yes,
In the fantastic forms; and where the pines,
Sweet censers of the land, perfume the air,
    Dolores. And to the melody of rustling leaves
The harp responds.
    Eduardo. Aside. Friend that I know so well.

Doña Eulalia.. It is the place for poetry and song.

Dolores. Did you discover any pretty shells?

Eduardo. O yes, I meant to tell you that I brought
For your collection some rare specimens.

Dolores. Thank you, Eduardo.

Doña Eulalia.   Let us see the shells.

Eduardo. They 're beautiful. I left them near the
      oak.

Doña Barbara. We 'll have Mateo polish them to-
      night.   *Exeunt.*

Enter Father Serra, Gov. Fages and Don Pablo.

Gov. Fages. I thought, Señor, you would agree with
      me.

Father Serra. And now you see that I was in the
      right:
I hope this judgment will have weight with you.

Gov. Fages. I really wished it could, your Reverence,
But what the viceroy says must be enforced:
Though I confess Don Pablo changed my views.

Father Serra. I 'm glad to hear you say that, Gov-
      ernor.

Gov. Fages. *Aside.* About his willingness to take a
      bribe.

Father Serra. Don Pablo, you exhibited those traits
That judges seem so seldom to possess.

Gov. Fages. Yes, your remarks were wise and per-
      tinent,
And your decision an impartial one.

Father Serra. I wish that you could be *alcalde* here.
Don Pedro, could you not create the post?

Gov. Fages. Why, certainly, but would Señor accept?

Father Serra. Although the office is beneath your
    rank,
And nominating you I surely owe
A deep apology; yet I would not
Have mentioned it, had I not heard you say,
You thought the office honored any man,
Especially in countries new as this.

Don Pablo. You owe me, Father, no apology.
You have suggested and have tendered, friends,
An honor due to merits hardly mine.
I 've always shunned the law as I have shunned
The restless city world. My happiness,
And that I would consult, lies mid the scenes
Of sea and pastoral sublimity;
My herds have been increasing rapidly,
And now that I shall soon receive the—

Gov. Fages.   Hush!

*Picks up stone and throws off. Exits and re-enters with a
wounded bird.*

I rarely miss my aim!

Father Serra. Taking bird. A cruel act.

Gov. Fages. That opportunity I could not lose,
For I was always good at throwing stones.

Aside. He noted not the incivility.

To Don Pablo. What is the bird?

Don Pablo.   A wood thrush, I believe.

Father Serra. Must these sweet singers be the prey
    of men?
Has our executive no better sport

Then to rehearse the wantonness of youth?
A broken wing. Be quiet, wounded friend,
I 'll help you—there is Doña Barbara.
I 've seen her save these injured birds before.

Exeunt Father Serra and Don Pablo.

Gov. Fages. Another word and Serra would have
     known
About that grant of land. I better warn—
No, he would be suspicious if I did:
For nearly three months it has been a risk,
It can continue so a month or more.   *Exit.*

Enter Dolores and Eduardo.

Eduardo. *Holding a rosary in his hand.* Why, Dolores,
I am not worthy of this sacred gift.

Dolores. I think you are. I knew you would be pleased
if I made a rosary for you.

Eduardo. I am, and I thank you, I thank you with
all my heart. It shall always be with me, and when I
count these hallowed and iridescent beads, your name
will ever be remembered in the prayers.

Dolores. Thank you, Eduardo.

Eduardo. Tell me the history of this lovely emblem
of the mysteries.

Dolores. The chain, a silver one, has been an heir-
loom in our family almost three hundred years,—

Eduardo. Wrought in the misty decades of the past.

Dolores. Its story is authentic. It held captive a
large and brilliant toucan, that Christopher Columbus
brought to court on his first return.

Eduardo.   O, valued relic of the great discovery.

Dolores.   The beads are from the abalone shells I found upon the beach.

Eduardo.   Touched by a sea Columbus never saw.

Dolores.   The cross—

Eduardo.   The sacred symbol of the Christian Faith.

Dolores.   Is from a piece of yellow sandal-wood brought from the Philippines.

Eduardo.   The navigator's dream.   You carved the cross and beads, Dolores?

Dolores.   Yes, Eduardo.

Eduardo.   Aside.   The rosary is blest.

Dolores.   Do you know, Eduardo, you seem worried of late.

Eduardo.   I am.

Dolores.   It is nothing serious, I hope?

Eduardo.   It seems so, but may not be.   *Aside.*   The letter is best—no—yes—

Dolores.   One of those conditions of the mind where confusion and indecision rule?

Eduardo.   Yes, yes, that is it.

Dolores.   Perhaps I can comfort you; let me act your confidant.

Eduardo.   Yes, I will confide—you will hear me—you will decide—and when you have heard what I have to say—judge me not harshly.

Dolores.   I could never do that; I know too well the mission of sympathy.   What is the trouble?

Eduardo.   It is—I—the Church must lose—I cannot speak—here—let my messenger speak for me.   *Starts to give letter to Dolores.   Suddenly notices the rosary in his left hand, which he gazes at, and then at the letter.* No, no, Dolores, I cannot tell you now! Wait, wait—yes, wait—forgive me for refusing to confide. *Starts to exit.* I am not ready, for I do not know my way.   *Exit.*

SCENE II.   ANOTHER PART OF THE RANCHO OVER-LOOKING CARMELO BAY.   MOONLIGHT.   JUNE 3, 1784.

Enter Doñas Dolores and Barbara.

Dolores. How marked the moonlight shadows seem
     to-night;
The cypress have their outlines well defined.
O, look upon the sea!
Doña Barbara.   The scene is grand.
How far the great Pacific is illumed.
Dolores. It is a stoup where beams may blessings
     take

For those in far ethereal abodes.

Enter Father Serra, unseen by stage.

Doña Barbara.   Where hang the pendants of a holy throne.

Father Serra.   That light the upward way of saintly souls
To immortality.   Well, children, what
Has brought you here?

Doña Barbara.   The view, your Reverence.

Dolores.   For this is our retreat where after prayers
We often spend a quiet leisure hour.

Father Serra.   No one could wish a better place to rest.
How small are we in this stupendous space.
O, marvelous the works of God: For us,
He has ordained one scene of beauty shall
Tread close upon some vanishing display;
So fades the sun in sunset glorious,
And from the dusk that masks the coming change
There is evolved a great mosaic dome,
Whose golden settings aid the silver moon
In lending to the earth a borrowed light.
Let infidels behold and then explain
How came the system so appropriate
To wants of man.   O origin divine.
My children, let my blessings be with you.   *Exit.*

Doña Barbara.   How deep, how reaching his philoso·
phy.

Dolores.   It is indeed.

Doña Barbara.   Tell me, Dolores, dear,

What do you think of Captain Alvarez?
Dolores. Now, Barbara, why do you ask?
Doña Barbara. Because—
Because—just this; when he is not with you
Or Governor Fages, he is with me—
Dolores. Has he—
Doña Barbara. No, not in love with me but then
I think he is in love with you.
Dolores. I knew
That long ago.
Doña Barbara. You did!
Dolores. Why, certainly.
Doña Barbara. Then he has told you so?
Dolores. He might as well.
Doña Barbara. Now this is news to me; and that is
why
He often comes appearing so in doubt
About what you must think of him. I thought
That probably he had offended you.
Dolores. He talks to you of me?
Doña Barbara. Of nothing else.
Your joys and sorrows, hopes and fears, are all
Upon the list of questions he has asked:
He takes an interest in all you do;
The story of your life I 've told him twice.
Dolores. How very tired you must become of him.
Doña Barbara. No, for I am amused, so artless does
He try to make the questions seem to me.
We must return; we 'll talk of this again.
Dolores. Go slowly in advance, and I will come
Directly after, now I want to think

A little while alone.

Doña Barbara.	As you desire.	*Exit.*

Dolores.	Eduardo seems so worried, but no doubt
He wished to tell of struggles for their rights.
He is so earnest when he speaks, and then
He takes the friars' troubles so to heart.
To love I 'm sure he never gave a thought;—
How often in the past I 've wished he would.
It could not be—no, it was of the Church.

Manuel.	*Without.*	Whoa, Concha.

Dolores.	It 's Don Manuel, returned.

Manuel.	*Without.*	Stay here until I find that narrow
	trail.

Enter Manuel.

What, Señorita, is it you I see,
So far from home at night and here alone?

Dolores.	It is not far away, Don Manuel.
We just came out, that 's Barbara and I,
To have a pleasant walk.	How came you here?

Manuel.	I left my escort a full league behind,
And started out to find the way alone;
I lost the trail, it was a lucky loss.
Is Doña Barbara with you?

Dolores.	Not now,
We were just going home, she is ahead.

Manuel.	Delay your going for a while.
I thought of you when on my homeward way.

Dolores.	In consequence I made you lose your way.

Manuel.	To end as this I would be lost again.
The subject was a most absorbing one,

And as I rode along I gave my thoughts
To dreamy reveries, and Vespers chimed
From sweet San Cárlos bells as shadows fell
And night stood commandant to fleeting hours.

When deeper shadows of the night o'ertake
In silent way the early evening hour,
Then soft and low the silver bells forsake
Their quiet vigil in the mission tower:
In rhythmic measure sound the silvery notes
As o'er the peaceful valley they vibrate;—
How tuneful sweet the holy music floats,—
While drowsy doves in sudden flight gyrate.
So in such twilights oft I take my way,
To pray at Vespers in the place where dwells
An absolution for our sins of day;
What consolation 'neath those saintly bells;
    And at my death I ask no greater boon,
    Than pass away as floats their sacred tune.

Dolores.   May you receive the blessing that you ask.
Manuel.   Yours is indeed a kindly wish for me.
I 've ever found you good as beautiful.
Dolores.   Señor, you really favor me beyond—
Manuel.   That is a pleasure, I could think of you
Forever.   Yes—I have to think of you;
I cannot nor I would not cast aside
Such pleasant thoughts, of such a pleasant theme.
Dolores.   Now do not worship me—
Manuel.   I do, I do!
Your graces ask a man's idolatry,

"Blow tuneful sweet the holy music floats
While drowsy doves in sudden flight gyrate."

For admiration is too poor a word.

Dolores.   Do you forget the other ladies here?
What of Carlota or Engracia?
Are Señoritas Isabel, Ines,
Or Rosa Dávila by you forgot?

Manuel.   I have no thought of others that are here.

Dolores.   You are in love—so blind to grievous faults.

Manuel.   The object of my love, I took the care
To find devoid of trying faults, before
I would allow myself to be enslaved.

Dolores.   Ah! so you studied up advantages

With cold and business-like alacrity,
And then—you fell in love.
Manuel. No, no! I— I—
Dolores. Yes, yes, you have acknowledged that was it.
Manuel. I did not need to study what appears
So broadly plain to every passer-by.
Aside. It seems the more I say the worse I plead.
Dolores. But do you ever stop to think that I
May love you not?
Manuel. I think it all the time.
Ah, you will never know how I have loved!
Dolores. I know you have, you need not tell me that.
So deep are your affections then for me?
Manuel. Strong as the strength of tidal waves, and
deep
As the unfathomed sea from which they rise.
Dolores. Were I a man, no woman would lay claim
To my affections so.
Manuel. Not being one,
You cannot measure then, the attribute.
Dolores. Of man's affections, oft I 've heard it said,
They 're not renowned for their fidelity;—
So long as woman will be beautiful,
So long will live and love inconstant man.
Manuel. But, Señorita, I 'm not such a man.
Dolores. Perhaps you 're not the only gentleman
That thinks of me.
Manuel. I thought that I was right!
Where is my rival then, that I may make
With him a fighting opportunity?
I 'd leave him vanquished on contention's field.

Dolores.   Provided you are the superior.

Manuel.   I 'd give a thousand *pesos* for the chance
To see with him who 's better in a quarrel!
Who is the man, and where does he reside?

Dolores.   I 'm not aware that there is one—

Manuel.   O then
My way is clear?

Dolores.   There may be two or three.

Manuel.   Once more do you   destroy my fondest
        hopes.
Yet why should I withdraw for others here?
What is my life that I should try to save
It for the good of a corrupted state
To trade away in service of defense,
So some ranchero man could say to me
"The señorita is to be my bride,
I 'm sure you 'll join in our festivities."
No, no! if I 'm to have my rivals then;—
Why tell them they must fight!

Dolores.   That must not be.
I would not have you go to such extremes,
Nor would I love the victor of a fight.

Manuel.   I did not think, a woman seldom does.
Then I will be the worst whipped of the two!
So say the word and I will not defend
My person or my honor in the least,
But meekly stand and let the biggest coward
Or braggart of the town, they 're both the same,
Exult in his imagined victory.

Dolores.   I do not have among my friends the kind
That you describe.

Manuel.   O, pardon me again!
I really did not mean it in that light.
Forgive me for the errors that I make.
    Dolores.   They do increase at most alarming rate.
Señor, I must return, I will be missed.
    Manuel. Permit me to escort you home?
    Dolores.   No, thanks,
For it is best I go alone.   Good night.
    Manuel. Show me the road or I will lose the way.
    Dolores. Here, this one to the right, I 'll take the left.
    Manuel. Eduardo 's here!
    Dolores.   What shall we do?'
        speak?
    Manuel.   No.
I would not have him learn that we 're so near.

Enter Eduardo.

Eduardo. Aside. How like a vision did the rosary
Recall to mind the cloistered walk of life.
    Manuel. I 'm fearful that my horse will whinney
        now.
Step carefully.   Is this the path?
    Dolores.   Yes, there;
The house is east of us a little way.
    Eduardo. Aside. How many things I seem to miss
        in life.
    Dolores. I 'll go the other path.   There 's Barbara!
I have not followed her—she 's coming back—·
The chaparrel is thick—we 'll have to stay
Until she finds I am no longer here.
My path is to the left, too far away

To reach without discovery.   Be still.

Eduardo.   Aside. It ever is the actor not the line.
He who creates, commands approval most.

Manuel.   I hope that she will not discover us.

Eduardo.   Aside. O, how romantic love must be to
    some.

Dolores.   I was most indiscreet to stop to talk.
I wish I had not stayed.

Manuel.   I 'm glad you did.
By being indiscreet I stole a joy:
Yet when invested with so many charms,—
A moonlit sea, a surf, and forest grand;
An air as balmy as the tropic night;
And then with one whom Nature made so fair
That when compared with her the scene is poor;
An opportunity as indiscreet
I can but hope will come quite soon again.
I 'll shield you from all harm, so trust in me.

Enter Doña Barbara.

Eduardo.   Aside. Are all men's lives so bordered by
    a love?

Doña Barbara.   Dolores! O, Dolores!

Eduardo.   ·   Who is that?

Doña Barbara.   Why, who are you?

Eduardo.   My name 's
    Ortega, who—

Doña Barbara.   Eduardo?

Eduardo.   Yes—O, Doña Barbara?

Doña Barbara.   Yes, have you seen Dolores?   She
    was here.

We were out walking and she strayed behind.

Eduardo. I have not seen her since devotion hour.
I came out for a walk and just arrived.

Doña Barbara. Well, we were here a little while ago.
No doubt she took the shorter way for home.

Eduardo. Quite possible. *Aside.* A path I never
take.

Doña Barbara. She must be home by now.

Dolores. Aside to Manuel. I wish I were.
I shall tell Barbara of this.

Manuel. Do not,
I beg of you, I 'm sure she 'd take offence.

Dolores. Here is an opening, I 'll run ahead. *Exit.*

Eduardo. Perhaps she walked along the beach.

Doña Barbara. No doubt.
Well, I will hurry back. Good night.

Eduardo. Good night.

Exit Doña Barbara.

Manuel. Aside. Here is my time to vanish in the
woods. *Exit.*

Eduardo. Ah, to destroy the letter as I did
On afterthought, was wisdom well employed!
No, I must be the man and to her face
Speak of my love, and not with craven pen
Disclose the story lips alone should tell:
He who 's afraid to brave his lady fair
With such a tale, is shadow to a man;
Unable to in danger great, defend
The woman he professes to adore.
No more of that! I 'll now declare to her

With all the polish of a cavalier,
That I, one of the great Ortega house
Of noble Spain, intended for the Church;
Will on acceptance of his heart and hand,
Renounce ambitions in that line of work,
And lay at his Dolores' feet, the wealth,
The strength of an undying love.   What 's that!
Who 's next to make a visitation here?

  Manuel. Without.   Whoa, Concha.   I must know
  more of the roads.

       Enter Manuel.

I wonder if he 's here?
  Eduardo.   Well, Manuel!
So you have just returned?
  Manuel.   And lost the trail.
I gave my horse the rein and found myself
Up by an old corral, where he was kept
Before I bought him of the don.   But you,
Once more out walking and absorbed in thought?
  Eduardo.   O, yes, it has become a fault with me.
  Manuel.   A pleasant habit rather than a fault.
  Eduardo.   Yes, 't is agreeable.   No incident
I hope arose to mar your ride?
  Manuel.   Except
That I was lost, each league had its delights,—
In fact, through those delights I lost my way.
  Eduardo.   I 'll set you right.
  Manuel. Aside.   I only wish he could.
I wonder if she 's angry with me for—
  Eduardo.   What 's this, a handkerchief?   Dolores—

Manuel.   Yes.

Eduardo. How do you know?

Manuel.   I only guessed at it.

Is not this place her favorite retreat?

Eduardo. It is. You càme with her some time per-
    haps?

Manuel. No, no, but I have heard her say it was.

Shall I return the handkerchief?

Eduardo.   I will.

O, how about that franking privilege?

What does the governor expect to do?

Manuel. I really cannot say. I spoke of it,

On which he smiled and would have answered me,

But then an orderly called him aside

And I forgot to mention it again.

Eduardo. There is a tale behind that cynic's smile.

Manuel. You are not just, the governor means well.

Eduardo. He is not just to us.

Manuel.   He tries to be.

Eduardo. Please do not say a thing like that, old
    friend.

Manuel. These troubles we should never talk about.

Eduardo. Yes, argument is sure to break the peace:

In wordy wars agreement seldom comes;

The ends oft fail to profit either side,

And only serve to rupture friendship's bonds

Or sunder ties which better close remain.

No doubt you will attend Don Pedro's fete?

Manuel. Indeed, I shall.

Eduardo.   Dolores will be there?

Manuel. Yes, why?

Eduardo.   O, I was only wondering.

Manuel. Aside. Fages was right. *To Eduardo.*
I must return, it 's late;
The governor is awaiting my report.
I wish you 'd show the way, Eduardo.

Eduardo.   .   There,
Ride o'er the knoll and then turn to the left,
From past the blasted pine the road is straight;
The lights will be your guide. I follow soon.

Manuel. All right, I 'll find the way. Good night. *Exit.*

Eduardo.   Good night.
My thoughts can need no goad to wander there
Within adobe walls, where glimmer lights
That throw a radiance around her form—

An æolian harp sounds.

The weird æolian! the wind is up;
I hear you, Harp, O, softly sound again!
Ah, music kindred of devoted love,
Speak unto those sweet sentiments that in
My ardent soul so struggle for response.
I know all nature does not sleep at night
For there are some who seek repose in day
That nightly watches keep; so I will watch,
And meditate, and dream and theorize,
While you, O Harp, companion, sing to me.
There, give to me the turbulent caprice,
The phantom that a violinist dreams:
Was ever music played and mastered so;
Your themes depict your versatility.
If she were only here so I could speak,

The beauties of the place would win my cause—
How happy I will be when hearing ' Yes,'—
And yet she knows it not.   What now appears?

Enter Father Serra, scourging himself.

Father Serra.   Aside. Sink in this sinful frame, re-
    proving scourge!
Destroy the evil there; make me more fair
In features of the soul so pure, so rare;
That God may look on me and turn away
With unoffended eyes.
Eduardo.   Aside.   His Reverence!
Look on your mentor and his saintliness:
The contrast comes again,—it 's ever near.
Father Serra.   Whom do I see, my sight is somewhat
    dim?
Eduardo.   Your Reverence, it is Eduardo here.
Father Serra.   What can Eduardo want so late at
    night?
Eduardo.   I stole away to meditate.
Father Serra.   It 's well;
A thoughtful mind alone would do as that.
To mend the future is to note the past,
For we can always find our errors there.
You came to me two years ago to-day?
Eduardo.   Why so it is, your Reverence, to-day.
San Carlos' fourteenth anniversary.
Father Serra.   Two things we should be very thankful
    for.
Be faithful to your Church and to your friends,
Work for humanity; and you 'll be blest.

Eduardo.   O, that, my Father, I shall never be:
I am too sinful, humble and unknown.
   Father Serra.   *Aside.* So humble now; marked is the
      saintly trait.
   Eduardo.   My future 's dark, my penetration 's poor.
   Father Serra.   Let not that be your grim discourager,
For penetration comes to those who seek.
My son, heed what advice the Father gives.
   Eduardo.   You speak to one unworthy of advice.
   Father Serra.   We 're all unworthy, son, and unto
      you
One most unworthy speaks; bear that in mind.
You 'll have dark ages in your youthful years;
I oft experienced that dismal state,—
Those rayless and depressing periods,—
Days when you 'll see no light but what reflects
From your distorted views: but struggle on
And never note the profit to yourself;
Our triumphs are not those that win applause,
So then expect it not, and ask it not,—
When you are dead if you deserved a thought
The world accords you praise; and that is right;
But recognition by your God exceeds
By far the honors gained from fellow-man;
We find in that the true divinity:
That was Saint Francis' rule, we 'll follow him.
   Eduardo.   Ah, Father, what a comfort are your words!
Now do I see my future in the light
Of understanding and of truth.   *Aside.*   Pass on!
You agonizing questions of the hour;
Away, Love, with your trivialities!

I want no more of you!   Pass on, pass on!
   Father Serra.   Yea, in your darkest moments let His
      works
That stand so visible, stand there to lead:
When you behold the high Sierra peaks
Remember, as you gaze, they ever point
To the abode of everlasting life!
Grace from the Hand above, to light the way;
Should be your prayer from this eventful day.

ACT III.

Curtain up on Father Serra and a neophyte choir.

Father Serra. My sons, now sing once more Saint
   Joseph's hymn.
Ignacio, lead off; sing slower though.
Fernando, let your bass be heard.   Commence.
Choir sing.

> *O let the world in duty bow,* •
>   *This is Saint Joseph's day;*
> *To him your humble prayers avow,*
>   *Afflictions he will stay;*
> *A sacred soul we kneel to now,*
>   *As Mass our Fathers say.*

Father Serra.   I see you have improved in singing this.
Jacinto and Ramon, the tenor 's good.
Now for the second verse, Ignacio.

Choir sing.

> *For with Saint Joseph as a guide,*
>   *From sin we shall be free;*
> *In him assistance does abide,*
>   *Our errors he can see;*
> *O, Fathers, help us to his side,*
>   *Confess we should to thee.*

Enter Father Noriega.

Father Noriega.   Praise be to God.
Father Serra.   Amen.
Father Noriega.   How
   well they sing.
Father Serra.   They do, indeed.   My children, you 're
   dismissed.

Exit Choir.

I 'm anxious that the choir shall know the hymn
By nineteenth of July, when monthly Mass
In honor of Saint Joseph shall be said.
   Father Noriega.   You 'll not be disappointed in your
      hopes.
   Father Serra.   If disappointment went no farther than
The learning of a hymn I would be glad.—
Our California I fear will not
Be fully under missionary rule.
   Father Noriega.   That end no doubt will be attained.
   Father Serra.   It may.
Still states against the Church are obstinate;
They take advantage of our principles.
   Father Noriega.   They know the priestly craft would
      not descend
To the low means its enemies employ.
   Father Serra.   This month my license to confirm ex-
      pires.
And I no longer can administer
The Holy Sacrament to these poor souls.
   Father Noriega.   I 'm sure that a renewal will arrive.
   Father Serra.   I fear 't will not. The propect 's also poor

For friars and we are so short of help;
And then this domineering of a man
Whose exit from the ranks was a mistake,
Is suffering indeed—but we must bear.
Old and infirm, my work is nearly done,
The evening of life brings me despair.

    Father Noriega.   This year has been a most unhappy
        one.

    Father Serra. Alas, my friend, what have I now tc
        show

For all my work?   Where is the legacy?

Last night I found upon the sandy beach
    An abalone shell, the sea had thrown
    From off the rocks, the place where it had grown.
That lustrous nacre as it lay to bleach,
Gave me a theme that I to all could preach;
    It was, ' How little are God's wonders known,'
    On every side so lavish has He sown,
Yet on we pass quite heedless what 's in reach.
Then sad became my thoughts there on the sand,
    While restless waves their nocturnes moaned to me;
For that bright pearl made by our Father's hand,
    Disclosed that I, of intellect so free,
Could at my death leave not one work so grand,
    As was that shell left stranded by the sea.

    Father Noriega. It is our lot to be content and work,
And in our aging years with sorrow look
Upon a life in futile efforts spent.
Here is Don Manuel.

Enter Manuel.

Manuel.   Good morning, Fathers.
Father Serra.   I 'm glad to see you, son.

Father Noriega.   Good day, Señor.
Manuel.   I 've brought a message to your Reverence.
Father Serra.   What says the governor, not, ' No,' I
     hope?
Manuel.   It 's with regret I say he has declined.
Father Noriega.   Again, yes, once again! we might
     have known.

Father Serra.   I 've been expecting that; but step
      within
And tell me what he said.   I 'll answer him.   *Exeunt.*

Enter Eduardo.

Eduardo.   O, how unbearable is argument
When your opponent is your wretched self.
I thought within the forest by the sea
That well-remembered moonlit evening,
That henceforth I would labor for the cross;
In that determination feelings ruled.
Shall I abjure intent of holy life? —
The chance I lose in youth I 'll not regain
To be ordained a Father of the Church;
For when our youth is past, we lose those years
So precious for the basis of great works, —
Then, to begin upon the rudiments
In middle life, is difficult to do, —
Still, still, with her I would not wish a change.

Enter Father Noriega.

Father Noriega.   My son, the governor received the
      note?
Eduardo.   Yes, Father, I delivered it to Juan,
Who later on reported it received.
Father Noriega.   He had it then before the captain
      came, —
Insulting us by disregarding it.   *Exit.*
Eduardo.   The Fathers have their trials as well as I.
O may I judge with those far-reaching views

And wisdom that is bought in man's estate!
What, here to-day?   I 'd rather be alone.

Enter Manuel.

Eduardo.   How are you, Manuel?
Manuel.   I 'm very well.
I hope you are the same?
Eduardo.   I am quite well.
Manuel.   Your looks do not confirm the statement
    though.
Eduardo.   In health I am the same.
Manuel.   But not in mind.
In you I 've read a strange perplexity.
Eduardo.   Well, yes, I have been worried some of
    late.
Manuel.   Forget the winter not, though summer 's .
    here.
Eduardo.   What may you mean by that, dear Manuel?
Manuel.   From what I 've seen I think you are in
    love.
Eduardo.   In love!
Manuel.   Exactly so, but it 's not strange—
Eduardo.   I do not know about that now, it is:
You never dreamed I 'd give the passion thought?
Manuel.   I 've had suspicions of the fact,—it 's sad.
Eduardo.   What, ah yes, so it is.   Is all love sad?
Come, tell me what you think about my case:
Is all love fraught with thought and argument?
You 've seen more of society than I,
And so must have some knowledge of its charm.

Give me advice and sympathy,—I need
The latter most.
> *Manuel.*   And so you love her then.
> *Eduardo.*   She 's now the inspiration of my life;

Why, Manuel, you do not know my love.
> *Manuel.*   Do you forget the Church has been your
> aim?
> *Eduardo.*   There, that has been my trial these many
> months;

I dread to leave the Fathers and the work,
And hazard fortune in a foreign craft.
In fact, I have not told his Reverence,
I was afraid that it would break his heart.
I am in doubt.
> *Manuel.*   It 's well you are in doubt.

Eduardo, I have been your life-long friend,
And therefore am commissioned by that right
To show Eduardo's follies to himself.
All youth must feel the sovereign power of love,
For it 's a trait that will assertion make,
But heed it not and it will die away,
A thing forgotten, just an episode,
Deserving not a memory or thought.
> *Eduardo.*   Forget—forget—and   wounded   as   I 've
> been?

I will forget when memory is dead.
> *Manuel.*   Bow not in such humility to it;

It is a fault to let a passion rule:
Beware or it will master you.
> *Eduardo.*   It has.
> *Manuel.*   And lead you stealthily to married state,

An outcome you forever will regret.

Eduardo. With her? that cannot be.

Manuel. O, but it will.
This love of yours seems strong, it is not so.
It 's but a ripple on a surface calm.

Eduardo. The ripple is an overwhelming flood.

Manuel. Besides she would not make for you—

Eduardo. Stop there.
For, Manuel, she lacks deficiencies.

Manuel. Well, that may be, but you are very wrong;
For Nature has selected some of us
To serve the Holy Apostolic Church,
And of that favored number you are one.

Eduardo. I thought so once.

Manuel. And you should think so now.
Your early plans and thoughts kept company
With all that 's grand and solemn in this life:
How often have you spoken of the time
When through the vaulted nave with aspergill,
You 'd walk to bless the congregation there:
Or in the many altar rites your hand
Would draw from the ampulla's sacred store
The unction of a soul. How often have
You hoped to rear in still more distant wilds,
Such sanctuaries as were builded here:
And yet these and the thousand other ways
In which a priest can be of lasting good;—
You 'd disregard for frail affection's tie.

Eduardo. Perhaps I have been wrong,—perhaps I
have.

Manuel. Why think of it, Eduardo, think of it.

Had you not better be a saintly priest
And walk a road of thorns in sanctity,
Than live the rich ranchero's life of ease?
I judge that 's the employment you would choose;
And when that life nears end you 'll have to say,
"I 've saved no souls, I 've not advanced the Church,
I have not preached the way my kind should die,
No, but I have accumulated wealth,
And on that profit rests a wasted life."
Ah, Miserere then will be your psalm!
Te Deum to your life you cannot sing.

    Eduardo.   You 're right, you 're right, you 're right.
    Manuel.   Let me recall
A former pictured future to your mind.
    Eduardo.   No, it is needless, for I see it now.
    Manuel.   Then you are growing wise.   Beware the
       bond,
Or life will be to you a field of tares.
Besides the greatest folly of it all
To try and win an unresponsive love.
    Eduardo.   "An unresponsive love!" why call it that?
    Manuel.   Because another has her heart.
    Eduardo.   What 's that!
You mean to say she loves another man?
    Manuel.   You speak as though you had no argument;
My good advice is thrown away.
    Eduardo.   O no,
I do appreciate what you advise;
But as I said, you do not know my love;—
It 's no mirage to fade when questioned close
But I would like to know who is the man.

Manuel. You did not talk like this when I returned.
Eduardo. I 've learned since then.
Manuel.   And you have yet to learn
You since learned little.
Eduardo.   Who's the man she loves?
Manuel. I do not like to tell you that.
Eduardo.   Come, come!
I will not have a rival in the town!
I shall engage myself this very eve.
   Manuel. *Aside.* I went too far. Now for the trag-
     edy.
Eduardo. Why do you hesitate? Speak out! Speak
     out!
Manuel. I 'm the one.
Eduardo.   Manuel. It 's you she loves?
This is too much! this is too much to bear!
Some other one, and I 'd have fought for her;
But you, against you I shall not rebel;—
You 've been to me too honestly a friend.
But are you sure she is in love with you?
   Manuel. It 's very plain.
Eduardo.   Where is the evidence,
Dear Manuel? I must be very blind;
I really have not seen or heard a thing:
She 's sure to tell me anything like that.
It could not be that you are wrong in this?
   Manuel. Quite unabashed you seem to doubt my
     word:
I told you that she loved me, that 's enough.
   Eduardo. It should have been, that was unkind
     of me;—

I did not doubt you, though. I 'm sick at heart.
But I 'm surprised she did not tell me this:
I 'll ask her why.
    Manuel.   Do nothing of the kind!
So take my word and let the matter drop.
    Eduardo.   Why, Manuel! why do you talk like that?
    Manuel.   Because I do not care to have it known.
    Eduardo.   Must then Don Pablo or his family
Know nothing of this love? That is not right;
You 've given me advice, let me advise;—
Inform her father of your happiness,
It looks suspicious keeping such a fact.
    Manuel. Suspicious! how? It 's nothing of the kind!
    Eduardo.   *Aside.* It does not seem that she has
        gone from me.   *To Manuel.*
But it will soon be known by accident,
Then what diversion would the gossips have.
    Manuel.   I wish you 'd please attend to your affairs,
And not concern yourself—
    Eduardo.   No, I will not!
If she accepted you, it 's my affair
To the extent of seeing it disclosed;
I 'll tell Don Pablo ere the day is o'er,
And also ask her why she told me not.
No stain shall ever rest upon her name
While I 'm her friend!
    Manuel.   Eduardo, you 're a fool!
You 've dreamed so long you are not practical.
Aside. I 've but myself to blame for all of this;
As yet from her there 's no encouragement.
To have her know I published such a thing

Would on the hearing warrant my disgrace.
Retreat?—no! Brave it out and see Fages.
Eduardo. Aside. No evidence—her failure to remark—
He is impulsive though and may be wrong—
The worst of all to try and hide the fact—
Such a solicitude—to speak so sharp—
No heart for one who suffered such a stroke—
That spirit 's born not of true fellowship.
To Manuel. Aha! I see! The light begins to break!
I did not think my friend would treat me so:
Why, what a bare-faced scheme.
  Manuel.   You do imply—
  Eduardo. · That you have lied to me.
  Manuel. What! *Draws sword.* No. *Sheaths sword.*
  Eduardo.   Strike! strike!
It will avail, because when I am dead
You will be free to push your cause along,
And try to win the love of her who now
Has not for you the shadow of regard!
Forget the winter! no, indeed, I 'll not!
You are the bitter winter of my love,
The frost that comes to blight my fondest hopes,
The warming rays of sympathy you 've not:
Go on your way, ally, you brought regrets.
As I said once to Love, away, away!
I say to you, begone, you treacherous
Deceiving prop of State's iniquity!
I want no interference from you here!
And mark you this, you 'll go!—though love did not.
  Manuel. Stop this tirade, sir, stop!
  Eduardo.   Why should I cease?

O, Friendship, what a champion you have
In Captain Alvarez, a servant high
In the opinion of the governor,
The friars' friend in California.

Enter Father Serra.

Oppose me!   Yes, I am just the one to let
You do a thing like that!   I 'll end you now!

Rushes at him.

Father Serra.   My son, my son!   What means this
    sinful act?
Do you forget the sacred lessons taught?
Are they in merit quite so poor as this?
I knew you both to be the closest friends,
I do not wish to see you enemies.
Manuel.   But I 'm afraid, no longer friend of mine—
I wrong him though, he 's not himself to-day.
If you have written, Father, I 'll return;
Don Pedro ordered me to hasten back.
Father Serra.   Go, hoping that these troubles will
    amend.
Here is my answer to the governor.   *Hands him a letter.*

Exit Manuel.

Eduardo.   An enemy, a man of artifice.
Father Serra.   I 'm pained to hear that, son; what did
    he do?
Eduardo.   He interfered with things he should not
    know,
And then to crown it all he lied to me;
It angered me to think that he, my friend,

Should act the part of a conspirator,
And in the transports of a sudden rage
I almost felt his life belonged to me.
Father Serra. O God, forgive your sinful soul. Go on.
Eduardo. O Father, note the errors that I 've
    made,
I can no longer stand uncertainty—
I cannot serve my God—I am too weak—
Absolve me, Father, from the hopes you 've held,
For I have dared or rather had to love.
Father Serra. Then you serve God, my child. Come,
    tell to me
The story of this new awakening,
That has occasioned you such loss of peace.
Remember, that confession comfort brings,
There is no rest so sweet to troubled minds,
Than knowing that the Father knows your trials
And can advise in sympathy with you.
Eduardo. Kind sympathy, what strangers we have
  been.   *Exeunt.*

Enter Father Noriega, Don Pablo, and Doña Babara.

Father Noriega. His Reverence is feeling better now;
But then, Señora, I am glad you came,
For he would like to have you make some more
Of that herb tea, it greatly strengthens him.
Doña Barbara. I 'm pleased to hear it was a benefit.

Enter Doña Dolores and Ignacio.

Father Noriega. Did you enjoy the ride, my child?

Dolores.   So much,
My Father, and of late I ride alone.
Father Noriega.   It is good exercise; but do not go
Too far away from home, the country 's wild.
Dolores.   O no, I 'm very careful in my rides.
Doña Barbara.   I 'll go and make the tea, your Reverence.
Dolores.   And I will go and help you, Barbara,
Father Noriega.   You better have Ramon get you
some herbs,
I do not think we have enough in store.

Exeunt Doñas Dolores and Barbara.

Father Noriega. You have a very pleasant home,
Señor.
Don Pablo.   My daughter is the comfort of my life,
And in her cousin Barbara she has
A kind companion in her youthful trials.
Father Noriega.   How sacred is a happy Christian
home.
Don Pablo.   The Church and home have close relationship.
Ignacio brought word the president
Was anxious to confer with me.
Father Noriega.   He is;
Inform the Father that Don Pablo 's here.

Exit Ignacio.

Don Pablo.   Ignacio is quite intelligent.
Father Noriega.   Yes, he has studied now for seven
years.

My duties call, Señor, I 'll leave you now;
His Reverence will be at leisure soon.   *Exit.*

Enter Doña Barbara.

Doña Barbara.   Ramon had not enough of herbs for
   me;
He went to gather some.
   Don Pablo.   Now, Barbara—
There 's something that I wish to speak about.
You know, we 'll not return to Spain and so
No doubt Dolores will be married here,
And there 's a point on which I 've been disturbed:
Who is the man that 's suitable for her?
Your care has been a watchful one?
   Doña Barbara.   It has.
   Don Pablo.   Because you know that ardent youth
   forget
That wisdom should have weight in love affairs;
From negligence grave indiscretions spring;
Keep note of those that pay her their respects;
Her husband must be of a noble line.
   Doña Barbara.   I keep informed, and then she tells
   me all.
Our family so ancient and so fair
Was ne'er by misalliance marred, and now,
We 'll not record beginning of the taint
While I may live to watch affinities.
   Don Pablo.   And all formalities must be observed.
   Doña Barbara.   I favor no romance when out of form.
   Don Pablo.   You 're true I see to Spanish pride of
   birth,

As you are to the ceremonials.
Reports are good of Captain Alvarez,
Somewhat ambitious and not rich, but still
He has the qualities that riches need
To make them well appear.   What other ones?
>   *Doña Barbara.*   Besides the captain there 's the brave
>   Miguel,

Who saved his friend Alférez Sal from death;
An Alvarado, they 're of noble blood.
>   *Don Pablo.*   I know of him, he is approved.   Who
>   else?

>   *Doña Barbara.*   Juan Castro 's next, the Mission
>   corporal.

His father 's a grandee of highest rank
And lives in Salamanca, I believe;
Juan cast aside his parents' proffered help
And ventured for his fortune in the west.
>   *Don Pablo.*   Accepted.   Whom does she admire the
>   most?

Or are there any more?
>   *Doña Barbara.*   Of course there are,

She 's loved by every one in Monterey;
Her fame for beauty like so many here
Has traveled down the coast to Mexico,
And many nobles of the capital
Have chosen wives in California.
>   *Don Pablo.*   Quite right.
>   *Doña Barbara.*   But every one must take
>   her smiles

And gracious favors share and share alike,
Her distribution 's marked by equity,

And none can say—"I am the favored one;"
They strive to gain more ground in her regard,
Still all are baffled in their best attempts;
I never saw young men so held aloof;
She is a master in that modest art.

    Don Pablo. The time will come when she will make a
        choice..   *Exeunt.*

       Enter Father Serra and Eduardo.

    Eduardo. I can partake of the Communion now.
It does not seem the chalice could contain
A blessing for my constant sinning soul.
Ah, Father, how can you forgive my sins?

    Father Serra. He 's yet to unforgive those that have
        erred,
Who in their hearts are sorry for their faults.

    Eduardo. I know, my Father, it is your great
        wish
For me to study and become a priest,
And to that end I have been most inclined—
Till Love, disturbing element, arose.

    Father Serra. It may be that and nothing more
        than that,
Again it may point out your course in life,
To marry and become a settler here.

    Eduardo. You will decide for me, your Reverence?

    Father Serra. Not I, my son, that must remain with
        you.

    Eduardo. It 's reason's will and passion's strength at
        odds,
They represent a duty and a love:

I 've read the lives of martyrs for the Faith,
I 'd like to die as died those stainless ones.
 Father Serra. How oft I 've wished that theirs would
  be my fate;
They spread the light—they spread the light afar.
 Eduardo. Opponent to this stands the layman's
  life;
She is my fate, for her I 'd gladly die;
I see myself a rich and happy don
And doing good to all within my reach—
My heart would be as kind as any priest's.
 Father Serra. Your mind is of the analyzing
  kind,
Not every one can concentrate his thoughts
As you have done—a splendid faculty;
Then the enthusiasm you possess
Will be in churchly work a priceless gift;
Therefore I counsel you, take time and think;
You have not told Dolores of your love,
Do not until you 're sure that course is best;
When you have settled on a choice, remain.
Again, as Manuel has said, she may
Not love you as you seem so sure she does;
Now if she does and you decide to stay
One of the laity, I shall assist
You all I can, and always be your friend;
I 'll see that you are well supplied with land;
But if you wish to study for the Church,
In San Fernando I will have you placed
The coming year, if I should live so long,
If not, the Fathers here will do for you.

Enter Ignacio.

Ignacio. Don Pablo has arrived, your Reverence.
Father Serra. Ah, yes, I would be pleased to see
him here. *Exit Ignacio.*
Eduardo. My Father, I 'll abide by your advice.
I thank you for your offers and your words.

Exit Eduardo.

Father Serra. So youth to manhood takes its stormy
way,
I had my trials, too,—and they were deep.

Enter Don Pablo.

Don Pablo. Good morning, Father.
Father Serra. I am pleased to see you, Señor. I wish
to talk with you about a rumor I have heard—that cer-
tain fugitive neophytes are in your employ; I do not
think you know they are converted Indians, and that
the rules forbid their working for other than Mission interests.
Don Pablo. I was in need of herders and some new
ones were sent from Monterey, but I did not know that
they were neophytes.
Father Serra. Who sent them, Señor?
Don Pablo. Governor Fages.
Father Serra. As I supposed.
Don Pablo. It could not be he knew they were—
Father Serra. He knew it. He sends soldiers to
bring back the runaways that through the influence of
their wilder brothers have been induced to desert the

Mission.   Don Pedro forces them to labor at the Presidio, getting their labor free of cost.   We complained of this months ago.

Don Pablo.   Is it possible!

Father Serra.   Señor Valencia knows nothing of this, as we thought.

Father Noriega.   Such acts are becoming every day occurrences.

Don Pablo.   Don Pedro must have known that it would be discovered.

Father Serra.   Did you request him for more help?

Don Pablo.   I merely made mention of my needs, and a few days later he sent the Indians with a note, saying I was free to use their services; but I shall return them to San Carlos this afternoon.

Father Noriega.   How many were there?

Don Pablo.   Ten in all; the governor sent more than I needed, but I suppose he thought as soon as I should receive the new addition, their assistance would be acceptable.

Father Serra.   You expect another grant?

Don Pablo.   Yes, it is the finest land in this vicinity; I petitioned the viceroy for it and the governor recommended the granting of the property.

Father Noriega.   May I ask where it is located?

Don Pablo.   It lies just east of us, running two leagues back and almost equal length from north to south; it is where the old rancheria stands; the tract is well wooded in parts with the manzanita and madrone.

Father Serra. What new misfortune has happened to us now!

Father Noriega. Who would have thought that he had gone to such extremes!

Father Serra. O what rascality!

Father Noriega. Infamous! It is infamous!

Don Pablo. Why, Fathers, what has happened?

Father Noriega. Again you are deceived.

Father Serra. How nefarious are the movements of this man.

Father Noriega. Fit subject for an anathema!

Father Serra. I 'll notify the viceroy at once!

Father Noriega. Do so by special courier!

Father Serra. Why, Don Pablo, are you a partner to this?

Don Pablo. I am at a loss to understand your Reverence.

Father Serra. This plot to steal the Mission lands.

Don Pablo. What! Mission lands! Steal Mission property?

Father Noriega. You have it now.

Don Pablo. Does this land belong to the Church?

Father Noriega. Certainly it does.

Father Serra. I must see the governor immediately.

Don Pablo. I understood it was unclaimed. He made no mention of it being Mission land.

Father Noriega. The land is ours, or rather held in trust by us according to the original Mission grants.

Don Pablo. Perhaps he does not know this.

Father Serra. Of course he does. If the land was

title free, why did he recommend the viceroy to make the grant? He, as the governor, is empowered to con-vey lands to settlers.

Father Noriega. He was afraid to take the responsi-bility.

Don Pablo. Fathers, I am astounded at these revela-tions.

Father Serra. Only yesterday afternoon I sent a message to the governor requesting him to deliver us some agricultural implements held in storage at Monte-rey, and later I forwarded a note, making inquiry about the neophytes we were just speaking of; Captain Al-varez brought reply that the governor would not de-liver the tools and he did not state his reasons why: we have done a little work at cultivation the past few months, but it 's trifling considering the extent of prop-erty that should be made to yield the Indians the living that 's required: I can now understand why he held them back, having this grant in view.

Father Noriega. As to the note about the neophytes, he paid no attention to it.

Don Pablo. Well, well.

Father Noriega. How long ago did you make appli-cation?

Don Pablo. Three months, yes, over that.

Father Serra. Too late.

Father Noriega. This is scandalous! See him and openly charge him with this villainy!

Father Serra. His intentions are to place within the hands of settlers all land he can possibly seize in the vicinity of this and the other Missions, thereby preventing extension of Church interests, then secularization will follow.

Don Pablo. I do not wonder at your feelings.

Father Serra. If the answer to our petition would only arrive, it might contain some encouragement to continue the fight with this unrighteous man. Is month to succeed month and no relief, no justice for the Californias?

Don Pablo. Then you await some movement in the south?

Father Serra. Yes, we had to make complaints.

Father Noriega. Proceedings hostile to our policy; but it is either appeal or refrain and see conversion stop and the Missions retrograde: but though we write, much is referred to the *Audiencia,* which is very slow in its decisions.

Father Serra. He takes advantage of the fact. He will yet pay the penalty of treason to the frontier church, and when he falls, will fall his followers.

Father Noriega. In plots, the more involved the more is solved.

Don Pablo. Is he not a good Catholic?

Father Serra. Only as far as the outward observances.

Father Noriega. Why, Pedro Fages and Philip de Neve have gone so far as to influence Bishop Reyes to announce his intention of forming the Missions into a custody, to be called "San Gabriel de California."

Father Serra. Which will be another step nearer secularization; as it is they succeeded in having a new *reglamento* passed that will greatly injure us.

Father Noriega. The custody principle is now in

force in Sonora, and has been so far most destructive to Mission property.   Fages takes such quiet means to accomplish his aims.

Father Serra.   And that is why we suffer so.   He assumes an enemy's most dreaded form, the part of the genial hypocrite, except when he becomes angry and forgets himself.   He wins your friendship and one not knowing him confides, and all the time he is considering your vulnerable points, and thus he molds his villainies in the sunshine of these advantages.   Of all villains in the catalogue he is the blackest knave who aims to crush the rule of Christian Faith, for when the Church is swept away, then falls the fabric of society, superstition rules and back to barbarism tends the age.

Don Pablo.   It would.   We should beware such men.

Father Noriega.   Beware the governor!

Don Pablo.   Fathers, I will think this over, and learn the best course to pursue; and I ask of you to say nothing but calmly await developments.

Father Serra.   That is difficult to do, but you may govern us.   We are convinced you are a friend of the Church, and it is best that you fully understand the policy of the Mission system.   Step within, and Father Noriega will show you documents relating to the Mission rights and privileges.

Don Pablo.   I should like to know these issues better than I do.   *Exeunt.*

Enter Eduardo and Ignacio.

Eduardo.   You say you saw Dolores.

Ignacio.   Yes, I left
Her with Señora Barbara.

Eduardo.   She here?

Ignacio.   Yes, and Don Pablo.

Eduardo.   He is here?   What for?

Ignacio.   I think it is about the neophytes.

Eduardo.   I 've been in the chaotic world so long
I quite forgot the issues of the day.

Ignacio.   The señorita asked for you.

Eduardo.   She did!
That 's kind in her.   How much I wish that we
Had never met.

Ignacio.   Did Don Eduardo speak?

Eduardo.   Just a reflection that, so note it not.
Why am I blaming her? that is not just.
Be cautious now, you 're in a state of grace:
It 's not her fault that she is beautiful.
She asked about, or wished to see me, which,
Ignacio?

Ignacio.   To see you, that was all.

Eduardo.   I once did think I was a man of will,
Now what a most deceiving thought.   But then
A stoic could not face these shadows long,   .
His character would need another name.
It stops at this.   The Father 's calling you.

Exit Ignacio.

The president's advice was very sound,—
I ought to know my way, of course I do,
I love her, and I cannot kill the fact:
How sweet she looked the other afternoon.   .
I 'll speak to her—I 'll speak—I shall—I shall!

Enter Dolores.

Dolores.   Aside.   Absorbed in contemplation as his
    wont.   *To Eduardo.*
Eduardo.
Eduardo.   Ah, Dolores, I am glad,—
I 'm very glad you 're here.
Dolores.   You are not well.
You 're overworked, you should not study so.
Eduardo.   Yes, you are right, I should not study
    so.
Dolores.   What is the subject you are studying?
Eduardo.   My study, I have longed to tell you that;
It is, Dolores, that which you should know—
That is—I started once before to tell—
I—I—well, I do not know how to start—
The subject, I have read, has always lacked
An adequate description; it 's a theme
Classed with the psychological—it 's grave—
And very few propose its lines aright.
I think—I will describe it later on,
When I have manufactured phrases fit
To dress description in the proper light:
You ask narration when I 'm least prepared.
Dolores.   The subject must be deep.
Eduardo.   Yes, very deep,
Too deep for me to fully comprehend.
Dolores.   Do promise me to study it no more;
This contemplation makes you pale and sad.
Eduardo.   It is a wearing theme, and I 'm advised
To give the subject up; it 's good advice.

Yes, leave such hidden things to older minds,
Age and philosophy do well combine.
Eduardo. But I can hardly think a sage engrossed
On such a youthful theme. It interests
The more in early life, one finds it hard
To cast the thoughts aside, yes, very hard.

Enter Father Serra and Don Pablo.

Father Serra. I wish you would not hasten to depart.
Don Pablo. I must, your Reverence, for pressing
    things
Demand my quick return. The neophytes
Is one of them, that needs a remedy.
Father Serra. I 'm glad to see you are intent on that.
Don Pablo. Yes, Father. Come, Dolores, we must go.
Eduardo 's well, I hope? Come visit us.
Good bye. Where 's Barbara? Ah, there she is.
Dolores. Now do, Eduardo, come and see us soon.
Eduardo. Thank you, Dolores, I 'll come. *Á Dios.*

Exeunt all but Eduardo.

Eduardo. Another declaration fallen flat.
It must be some high power is guiding me,—
That unforeseen great destiny of man,—
Or else the mind 's embarrassed by the show
Of circumstance, and fails to make the point.
If she were swayed for me as I for her,
Then what a hopeless wreck she would become.
I will not try again, so fare you well,
My dearest friend, until I know my way:

Yet if I tell her of my longing love,
Suppose she scorns my humble offering—
The Padre said that she might not return
The deep affection that I feel for her,—
The thought is fearful when I think of it—
It 's maddening!   I could not stand the shock!
'T would kill me, Father, it would kill me!

Bells ring for Angelus.

ACT IV.

SCENE I. EXTERIOR OF THE OFFICIAL DEPARTMENT
AT SAN CARLOS, AFTERNOON. JULY 14, 1784.

Enter Father Noriega, Gov. Fages, Manuel and Ignacio.

Gov. Fages. I should like to see the president.
Father Noriega. He is engaged.
Gov. Fages. I notified Don Pablo to meet me here,
has he arrived?
Father Noriega. I do not know. Have you seen
him?
Ignacio. No, Father.
Manuel. A vessel came to port last night.
Father Noriega. Indeed! A holiday for Monterey.
Was there mail for us?
Manuel. Yes, it will be over soon.
Father Noriega. Notify the president the governor is
here, and that a vessel has arrived.

Exit Ignacio.

Gov. Fages. Is he sick?
Father Noriega. He 's always ill, but ever is at work.
He 's with his secretary now.
Gov. Fages. Drafting complaints about the mean-
ness of the State? It 's his regular occupation.

Father Noriega.   How unjust you are.

Gov. Fages.   Well, we will let that rest.   Who rode up?

Manuel.   The ladies, I am sure.   I 'll go and meet them.   *Exit.*

Gov. Fages.   Yes, there is Don Pablo.   I will join him.   .   *Exit.*

Father Noriega.   What insolence in misplaced authority and domineering in a uniform.

Enter Father Serra.

Father Serra.   I 'm told Don Pedro is here.

Father Noriega.   He just left me as you were coming out.

Father Serra.   How is the governor?   Well, I hope.

Father Noriega.   Irritable and insolent.   Señor Valencia and ladies just arrived.

Father Serra.   Indeed, I shall be glad to see them.

Father Noriega.   The governor said he notified Don Pablo to meet him here.

Father Serra.   He must have had some purpose in that.

Father Noriega.   Do you suspect?

Father Serra.   The grant?

Father Noriega.   I think the vessel brought the grant.

Father Serra.   That is it! he is here to officially notify me of the transfer.

Enter Ignacio.

Ignacio.   A soldier brought this packet from Monterey, your Reverence.   *Exit.*

Father Serra. Our mail. There is no communication from the viceroy—I tremble for us now—our petitions and complaints have not been acted on.

Father Noriega. Courage.

Father Serra. Here 's one from the Guardian. *Reads.* "A tract of land has just been granted to one Don Pablo Valencia, of Monterey, concerning which I have made an important discovery."—Fages succeeds!

Father Noriega. Be calm! Read on.

Father Serra. Reads. "For being desirous of knowing the location of the proposed grant, I compared the recommendations of Governor Fages with your last report on the lands of your district, and what was my surprise to find the tract included within the limits of Mission property, then I discovered that the governor's arguments were false and misleading, I tried to have the grant annulled, without success; the viceroy does not seem to understand the situation."

Father Noriega. As I suspected!

Father Serra. What infamy!

Father Noriega. Is there no hope for us?

Father Serra. Reads. "I shall bring the matter before the *Audiencia,* so gather evidence and send it to me at once. The petitions and complaints about Governor Fages' management that you forwarded last March, are being considered, favorably or not, I cannot say. The vestments Father Cavaller requested—"other matter.

Father Noriega. We have no evidence.

Father Serra. We must seek for it. I shall have an interview with Señor Valencia to-day.   *Exeunt.*

Enter Doñas Dolores and Barbara.

Dolores.   Invited oft, yet he remains away.
Doña Barbara.   He surely lacks the wish of seeing
friends.
Dolores.   Why even here we do not see his face.
Doña Barbara.   No doubt he has so much to do; you
know
He keeps accounts and helps in many ways.
Dolores.   That is not it, for he has kept accounts
A year or more.   We must go deeper still.

Finds book on chair.

Eduardo's book of prayer I gave to him.
The Aves and the Paters, blessed prayers,
Disclose the secret of his strange neglect.
Doña Barbara.   You have discovered it.
Dolores.   Devoted youth,
Your time is well assigned.   Forgiven now.
Doña Barbara.   Yes, that is it, for soon he hopes to
leave
For Mexico, to study for the Church:
His plans are good, I wish him all success.   *Exit.*
Dolores.   And so do I; but then—what might have
been.—
How opposite in character they are,—
Eduardo's good, I hope he will be blest.

Enter Eduardo unseen by Dolores.

Eduardo.   *Aside.*   Dream of me, friend, and dreaming
wish me well.

One looks and then her beauty must admit,
  For to deny would but the truth evade;
  I better speak, abjure the cloister's shade
And in her care my happiness commit.
A picture there, I never shall permit
  From loved Carmelo memories to fade.
  Yes, shun the cowl and play the serenade!
As acts the cavalier yourself acquit!
Stop—stop—do I forget I said farewell
  To meet no more until I saw the light
Of understanding 'lluminate my way?
My passions master me! my soul compel!
  Temptation hold! I 'll not! God guide me right:
To Nocturnes, Matins, Mass and Vespers pray. *Exit.*

Dolores. O, holy book, a solace ever be,
And unto him bequeath, who reads your prayers,
The kindest wishes from a constant friend. *Exit.*

Enter Gov. Fages and Don Pablo.

Gov. Fages. Don Pablo, you have been most for-
    tunate;
Here is the grant, you 'll find it quite correct.

Hands him a deed.

Don Pablo. I thank you, Governor, you are most
    kind—
Gov. Fages. No thanks, Señor, no thanks, I beg of
    you.

Enter Fathers Serra and Noriega.

Good Father, have you heard the welcome news?
Don Pablo 's now at liberty to use
The rancheria tract, it 's splendid land.

    Father Serra.   I would congratulate him if he had
An honest title to the property.

    Gov. Fages.   What do I hear!   The deed, Señor.   See
        this.
You know the signature.

    Father Serra.   It 's genuine.

    Gov. Fages.   O, I supposed you 'd say I forged the
        name.

    Father Serra.   We had a prior claim.

    Gov. Fages.   How 's that?
        O, yes!
A visionary claim!   I heard of it
Some years ago; yes, many years ago.

    Father Noriega.   Aside to Don Pablo.   I 'm glad our
        president can have this time
To show the governor what he has done.

    Don Pablo.   I think Don Pedro will recall the grant,
When is made known the error of the act.

    Father Serra.   So distant was the time you thought
        our claim
Of slight account, and so you made it out.

    Gov. Fages.   Well, what 's this all about, do you ob-
        ject?

    Father Serra.   I do object; the grant is most un-
        just.

    Gov. Fages.   O, that 's in keeping with your princi-
        ples—
To always take exception to my acts.

Father Noriega.   Don Pedro, do you wish to speak of
  this?

Gov. Fages.   I 'd like to hear about that prior claim,
That flimsy pretext for a churchly deed.

Father Noriega.   Then please respect the age that
  bows that head:
Your tones are rough, your speech is rude, refrain.

Gov. Fages.   I meant no disrespect.

Father Noriega.   I thought you did.

Father Serra.   The Church is pledged to guard this
  property,
Because the aborigines, who are
The rightful owners of the soil, became
The willing converts to the blessed Faith,
And placed their future and their trust in us.
This land is to afford them Christian homes,
When they are civilized to that extent.

Gov. Fages.   The viceroy thought the granting of the
  land
A step in progress, therefore very wise.

Father Serra.   He thought it wise? you say, he thought
  it wise?
Perhaps he did, on strength of your report:
But do you think the viceroy such a man
To grant this land away and knowing what
The Mission Fathers meant to use it for?
No, that official is too honorable:
Use these broad acres for a rich man's kine
To fatten on for his exclusive gain?
Where is the virtue in such narrow views?
He 's not the man to aid rascalities:

Can God's productive soil be put to use
In ways more suitable than to assist
The toiling, homeless and down-trodden poor?
    Gov. Fages.   Am I to always ask you what to do?
I 'm here to see this country colonized;
Has not Don Pablo worked to help the place?
I 'm sure he feels the want of some reward;
And justice should be given when it 's due:
So let the Indians go another place.
    Father Serra.   You prate of justice, how grotesque
        the forms
It can assume when you administer.
This grant 's a specimen of what you serve,
And the deserting neophytes you sent
To work as peons on Don Pablo's place,
Is but another instance of the kind.
    Gov. Fages.   Converted Indians! Now, how was that?
I take but little notice of the men.
    Father Serra.   Neglect of wrongs, conspiracies and
        thefts,
Make the administration prominent.
    Gov. Fages.   Insult the government and all concerned!
    Father Serra.   Insult the government!   Impossible;
I could not do a thing like that; it 's past
The touch of satire, insult, or of jest;
When truth becomes an insult then to prayers.
What! is this northern territory small?
Have we no settlers here to venture forth
When wishing to acquire new estate,
Or must the Church be always pioneer?
And when the time for its reward has come

In seeing savage proteges have homes,
Wherein the Crucifix its lessons teach;
The government steps in to wreck it all,
And give the world to understand, the Church
Is an accomodating deputy,
To venture in the wilds and pave the way,
So an ambitious State when all is well
Can grandly wave its servant to the rear,
And pose before the world—a power divine.

    Gov. Fages. I understand the Church should be
    maintained,
With due respect and in a proper sphere.

    Father Serra. Then, why do you persist upon your
    course?
I 'll tell you why you are the wrecker here,
It 's not to aid the welfare of the Crown;
It is because there lives in you the hope
To see Fages a little higher up
In politics—a slightly greater man.

    Gov. Fages. Were you but less in years I 'd answer you!
The king—

    Father Serra. Name not his majesty again!
Your old excuse, you represent the king;
If so, I represent His Holiness,
The supreme Word of an undying Church,
A man infallible, beside of which
The power of kings and grasping satellites
Can never hope to stand.

    Gov. Fages.   What 's that, you say!
Do you defy the king? our gracious king?

    Father Serra. O, do not aim to turn the subject so,

And try to cast upon me treason's stain;
You know I honor him, I always have;
The king is great, God save his majesty!
He cannot, though, attain the dignity
Or greatness of His Holiness, the Pope:
It is the king's misfortune we bewail.
    Gov. Fages.   Misfortune!
    Father Serra.   Yes, his trial, that he should
       have
For the administration of his laws,—
Such poor interpreters.
    Gov. Fages.   Now this must stop!
I come, I bow, I speak, I am abused.
    Father Serra. Don Pedro, you are ever welcome
       here,
E 'en though your bow is not an humble one;
The speech you make is not a gentle one;
And what you call abuse is justice served.
It 's a reproach upon the State that we,
The pioneers of California,
Who have spent years of toil and suffering
To build this wild and frontier country up,
Must in our aging years waste precious hours
To haggle for our just and lawful rights;
And every day we live, to know that one
Is near, with crafty, cruel, dark intent,
Quite ready on the opportunity
To mutilate or steal our recompense.
It is a shame, a most degrading shame!
    Don Pablo. O, Fathers, Governor, do pardon me,
I would attempt to place this matter right:

The governor assisted me to get
A title for this property, for it
Was·my request that urged him for the grant;
And Governor, I thank you for the work;
I 'm sorry that this trouble has occurred,
And there remains a duty to perform,
To deed the land again, so I 'll assign
All right and title to the Fathers here.
    Gov. Fages. Why, why! Don Pablo, this will never
        do;
It is an act for which there is no call;
No, no, keep it—I can not—I shall not
See fertile lands so lost upon a whim!
    Don Pablo. No, Governor, let it be set aside
For uses of the Church, they need it most.
I know you 've spoken for my benefit;
Thanks for your interest, but it must go
To those who hold the right, the prior claim.
    Gov. Fages. No, keep the tract! The Church shall
        not regain .
This land! entitled to the soil or not,—
The State is master of this colony,—
I 'll crush the—
    Don Pablo. Raise your hand against the Church,
Fages, and you remain no friend of mine.
Our ministers have suffered far too much,
And all the reparation man can make
Will not repay them for the good they 've done
Nor compensate them for the bitter trials
That they have undergone so many years.
I want no more of this disputed tract!

It 's Mission property, and with the Church
It shall remain!

    Gov. Fages.   O, then, if you insist—

    Don Pablo.   I do, your Excellency.

    Gov. Fages.   Then let them
Retain the land.   I 'll make the papers out
As soon as we return to Monterey.

    Father Serra.   Accept the thanks of all the friars, sir:
I 'll speak for them and though our humble thanks
Are all that we can give, you will be blest.

    Father Noriega.   You have displayed the spirit of the
        just;
We 're glad to see the Church has yet a friend
In California.

    Father Serra.   Praise God for that.

    Gov. Fages.   And *frailero* will 1 now be termed.

    Father Noriega.   It 's my regret you cannot merit that;
        Instead *El Oso* seems to please you most.

    Father Serra.   Thanks to Don Pablo we have justice
        now,
And I will notify the Guardian.
But what is Mexico to do for us?

    Father Noriega.   Though all 's in doubt we 'll pray
        they end as this;
From what the letter said we soon may know.

    Father Serra.   I hope the gentlemen will stop till eve,
So to attend the Vesper services.

    Don Pablo.   We will remain, your Reverence, and then
The governor and party go with me
To Rancho del Carrasco as my guests.

    Father Serra.   I am exhausted, let us go within.

Don Pablo, come, I wish to talk with you.
Now let me take your arm, your Reverence. *Exeunt.*
 Gov. Fages. Aside. I 'm glad he thinks I did it for
 his good.

Enter Manuel.

Manuel. Well?
Gov. Fages. Well?
Manuel. What can be done?
Gov. Fages. ˙ Nothing.
Manuel. Nothing!
Gov. Fages. Certainly.
Manuel. But something must be done!
Gov. Fages. Why so?
Manuel. I marvel you are cool.
Gov. Fages. I 've no reason to be otherwise.
Manuel. We 'll lose all! Must my greatest hopes
vanish when there 's a possibility of realization?
 Gov. Fages. I can find another—
Manuel. Another!
Gov. Fages. There are a thousand choice selections in
the land.
 Manuel. My love is not so easily transferred.
Gov. Fages. What are you talking about?
Manuel. This occurrence.
Gov. Fages. It will not affect your love affairs; it
will soon be forgotten.
 Manuel. Indeed, I rather think they feel too grate-
ful for the timely act.
 Gov. Fages. Why, then they 're satisfied. What more
can they ask?

Manuel. She 'll marry him! That will be his reward, while I who worship—

Gov. Fages. Stop. Tell me what you are talking about.

Manuel. This incident, of course.

Gov. Fages. Specify, specify.

Manuel. Dolores and Don Miguel.

Gov. Fages. I was referring to a tract of land.

Manuel. Why, have n't you heard that Miguel Alvarado saved Dolores' life?

Gov. Fages. No. When I left to walk with Valencia we spoke of land matters. I hope you are not sorry her life was saved.

Manuel. I bless the name of Don Miguel, but what becomes of me? she, woman-like, will take the sentimental view and marry him.

Gov. Fages. How well you have it planned. How did it happen?

Manuel. Jose, the *vacquero*, told her of some rare ferns and wild flowers growing in a cañon of the Sierra Santa Lucias, and yesterday she rode there alone to gather them,—a hungry mountain cat—a shriek—a swoon—my rival with a gun completes the stirring episode. He happened to be hunting that sheep-stealing animal.

Gov. Fages. And you have lost a bride, and he has saved his second life this year. Noble fellow! He well deserves reward.

Manuel. It was rather the hand of God than that of Don Miguel.

Gov. Fages. No doubt he was an instrument.

Manuel. The greatest hero is the knowing volunteer. What can be done? I cannot have my romance ended so,—send me away! No! send him away; that leaves the field to me,—that's it!—that's it! Do not allow him an hour in town, dispatch him to San Juan Capistrano on a mission to their Reverences, Mugártegui and Fuster.

Gov. Fages. You forget he is a civilian. Now if you were Don Miguel and Don Miguel—

Manuel. Don't mention him again! Had I his opportunity?

Gov. Fages. Come, now. Woman's gratitude does not always take a sentimental course. Don Pablo would not accept the land.

Manuel. What! It's his.

Gov. Fages. The president raised such strong objections he is going to give it up.

Manuel. Is it becoming so the friars rule in Monterey?

Gov. Fages. I did what I could to prevent it, but Don Pablo ruled; he insisted that the land should be given to the Church, in fact, he demanded it: I had to humor him.

Manuel. Another misfortune! We are losing influence.

Gov. Fages. I think not. I presume he thought the grant would be revoked on pressure from the Guardian, so to keep the peace he gave it up.

Manuel. Will not the president formulate this land business into a complaint?

Gov. Fages. Let him do it; where are his proofs that I misrepresented anything? I worded that recommendation too carefully. His complaint will be listened to, smiled at, referred to the *Audiencia*, and when they decide it was an unintentional error, about five years will have passed.

Manuel. An incident subject to the process of continuence.

Gov. Fages. Convenient. How seldom do we see your friend.

Manuel. Yes, but why, I cannot understand.

Enter Doñas Dolores and Barbara.

Dolores. Governor, you have missed something.
Gov. Fages. What is that?
Dolores. A fandango.
Manuel. You have been dancing, Señorita?
Dolores. Yes, I know the governor likes the dance.
Gov. Fages. Indeed I do. Why did you not tell me?
Dolores. Barbara thought you busy, your Excellency.
Gov. Fages. Doña Barbara, my cares will never be so pressing that I cannot lay them aside to attend a fandango, in which the Señorita is a participant.
Manuel. Or I. *Aside to Doña Barbara.* You are very cruel.
Doña Barbara. I am sorry, but you always seem so interested in military affairs I would not dare to interrupt.
Manuel. Señora, dare anything in such events.

Enter Doña Eulalia and Don Pablo.

Doña Eulalia. To Manuel. Captain, you are very partial to the demands of state.

Manuel. To my detriment I am.

Doña Eulalia. Most decidedly.

Manuel. I know it, I miss everything, always have, always will; everything has gone wrong; the governor is losing, I am losing; I never spent so unfortunate a day.

Don Pablo. Dolores, you should not dance so much.

Dolores. I am not tired.

Gov. Fages. Dancing is a healthful exercise.

Don Pablo. I believe in encouraging it, but one must be moderate.

Manuel. Who was the partner, Señorita?

Dolores. Juan Castro. He is a very clever dancer.

Doña Barbara. The best fandango dancer in Mon-terey.

Manuel. Aside. Ah, he is! Another rival! This is going too far! *Aside to Gov. Fages.* Governor, this must stop.

Gov. Fages. To Manuel. What is that?

Manuel. This corporal dancing with Dolores. Send him away.

Gov Fages. Certainly, I can transfer him to Mission San Antonio.

Manuel. That 's not far enough, send him to San Louis Obispo; Father Paterna will welcome him.

Gov. Fages. You command his destiny.

Manuel. Let him dance with the Indians for a change; as for Alvarado, I will challenge him at the first opportunity—no, I 'll not wait for that—I 'll make one I 'll—

Gov. Fages. Injure him and you injure yourself.

Manuel. What am I to do? Stand by and see this line of followers pay court to her? It seems my list of competitors has no end—a new one rises up at almost every hour to herald some heroic deed. Why, even Eduardo is likely any day to tell her of his love.

Gov. Fages. Do not become jealous.

Manuel. I 'm not,—but—

Gov. Fages. I see you 're not. Let them do heroic deeds that merit great applause. You forget I am behind you. I am still Don Pablo's friend and I never lose an opportunity to talk for you. Her father will have the choosing of her husband. They who lack influence also lack advancement.

Manuel. She 'll not be forced to take another's choice.

Gov. Fages. Failure I never recognize until success is irretrievable. *To Dolores.* Señorita, I heard of your escape, a narrow one; you should not venture so far alone, we cannot afford to lose you.

Manuel. Aside. No, nor lose you in any other way.

Dolores. I shall never ride so far again, unattended.

Gov. Fages. Aside to Doña Eulalia. Leave the young people alone awhile.

Doña Eulalia. Yes, you go first.

Gov. Fages. Señor, I should like to speak with you about some property yet unclaimed in the Pueblo of San José.

Don Pablo. Will the ladies excuse us?

Doña Eulalia. Certainly, Señores.

Exeunt Gov. Fages and Don Pablo.

Manuel. Aside. Now they are gone, and if the other two would only go.

Doña Eulalia. Do you not wish you were in Spain again, where savages and wild animals are unknown?

Dolores. No, I like California.

Manuel. Aside. Sensible girl!

Doña Eulalia. I am a lone exception.

Doña Barbara. So you are anxious to return?

Doña Eulalia. I long to see the lovely gardens of

dear Spain once more. This place is too new, I like a country that has some evidence of history, wealth, and power.

Manuel. Aside. I 'll make capital of this and bind her in a common bond of sympathy. The Señora is our foil. Enthusiasm, announce your admiration in ringing eulogies.

Dolores. How does the governor regard your views?

Doña Eulalia. I am sorry to say he desires to remain. Are you not anxious to return, Captain?

Manuel. For me, I would rather be identified with a new and coming land than live 'mid the conservative relics of moldy and moss-grown towers. 'Adventure' is the Spaniard's watchword that impels him to seek for wealth, authority and fame, in countries that savages possess; and by that spirit heroic exploits stand achieved. A greater land requests attention now; and yet the people of the East live enwrapt in the mightiness of their existence, forever failing to recognise the fact there grows a western world. But if the East is opulent and strong; the West, enriched by Nature is rising as a power. If the East is beautiful; the West not only has that excellence, but far surpasses it by being vast, marvelous, and sublime. If the East has a history; the West, though new, is making one and one that any state might well be proud to have. Give me the West, the pushing, progressive, and ever-assertive West!

Dolores. Bravo, *Capitan*, speak well of the West.

Doña Eulalia. For some this country offers great advantages, but I feel out of place; my happiness is centered in Madrid. Come, Señora, I want you to show me the village of the neophytes; I have never visited it.

Doña Barbara. Certainly. We 'll leave you to your-
selves awhile.

Manuel. Aside. But they are kind.

Dolores. You 'll find the village quite an interesting
sight.

Exeunt Doñas Eulalia and Barbara.

Manuel. Aside. How bountiful was Nature with her
    gifts;
In one long life we meet like her but few:
I 'll wait no more, I 'll know my fate to-day.
Ah, Señorita,—I—I—

    Dolores.   Well, Señor?

    Manuel. I need advice.

    Dolores.   Indeed, now what about?

    Manuel. I—will you counsel me?

    Dolores.   Perhaps, Señor,
I am not qualified—

    Manuel.   O yes, you are!

    Dolores. Well, now, what would you have advice
    upon?

    Manuel. Avowal must come first—I am in love.

    Dolores. Why, that is news to me. Who is she now?

    Manuel. I will reserve the name a little while.'

    Dolores. But what can I advise in love affairs?

    Manuel. Just this, a little thing, though hard to do:
When I propose, what method 's best to take?
Shall I to her in rhyming cadence speak,
Or turn my words into poetic prose?
For I would have my play without a flaw.

In fact I 'll have to use the greatest care,
So says the governor, and he must know.
    Dolores.   Then you 've been hunting for advice before?
    Manuel.   O no, no, the remark was casual.
    Dolores.   How can I tell you what to say to her
Unless I know the kind of girl she is?
Besides—you know the sweetest words are best.
    Manuel.   Then teach me in a way that 's general.
    Dolores.   That would not do, each case is different,
And with a just severity demands
Perfection in announcement of a love.
Describe her first so I may know the way.
    Manuel.   She might be angry if I pictured her.
    Dolores.   I promise not to tell.   Does she live here?
Of course she does, so just tell me her name;
'T will save description for I know them all.
    Manuel.   A secret that must be, her home and name.
    Dolores.   Describe the mystery, I 'm curious.
    Manuel.   Well then, prepare to be astonished by
Her many gracious charms, for they 're unmatched.
I 'll start upon her disposition first;
O that in her is incomparable;
I see the promise of a happy life;
She has a time-defying patience that
No matter how monotonous the hour,
Her rare propensity will master it:
Then when she smiles you see how lovable
Her nature; for there 's much in woman's smile;
Her glance so soft, 't would wreck the strongest will
That said he 'd love her not.   And then her voice—
Be it in song or conversation low,

All listless moments vanish on the sound,
For harmony enriches every word.
    Dolores. So far as you have gone, she 's marvelous.
O, yes—what is the color of her eyes?
    Manuel. Her eyes have the ascendency o er all,
And like most Spanish maidens they are black;
But there their rivalry with her must stop;
For though her eyes are dark they 've other charms
That far surpass the spell that others have;
They 're brilliant as the gleam of diamonds,
But they unlike the diamonds are not cold;
She need not use her voice for they speak out
More eloquently than magnetic speech.
    Dolores. I am becoming jealous of this girl.
    Manuel. Her hair, her face, her hand, her foot, her
      form,
Need long descriptions which I hope you 'll waive
For want of fitting words,—but this I 'll say,
She has been so endowed, that art would fail
In trying to delineate the truth:
Kind Nature left in her a masterpiece.
    Dolores. How beautiful she is. How you must love.
    Manuel. As loves a Spanish cavalier.
    Dolores.   Enough!
That answers all demands.
    Manuel.   So in what way
Must I propose to run no chance of loss?
    Dolores. A Spanish cavalier does not require
Such information in his love affairs.
    Manuel. But might there not arise to kill my plea,
Some rude, ill-placed, incorporated word?

Dolores.   It often does,—but this advice is dear.

Manuel.   Though it would take the fairest gems in
       Spain,

Or anything more stable than the gold

That tints and ornaments the sunset clouds,

I 'll seek for it, and finding, pay the debt;

Yea, teach me words that will insure success,

That on their utterance, ' Yes', is reply,

And I 'll endow you with a just reward:

You 've promised me and I have told you all.

Dolores.   What, all?

Manuel.   O no, I could not tell you all;

I 'll not attempt the indescribable.

Dolores.   *Aside.*   O can it be that this is his revenge,

Due for my not encouraging his suit?   *To Manuel.*

You told me once that you admired me.

And yet—

Manuel.   I do with all—

Dolores.   What 's that! you do?

And love another, as you so declare?

Now that admission is a cruelty

To her, she has my deepest sympathies;

Suppose I tell her what you 've said to me.

Manuel.   O, she would not be angry in the least.

Dolores.   You thought she would when first I ques-
       tioned you:

How marvelous a nature she must have.

Manuel.   She is to me almost a miracle.

Dolores.   But are you never jealous of your love?

Manuel.   I am at times, there 're rivals for her hand.

Dolores.   A Spanish cavalier with rivals, no!

Where is your rapier? are you afraid?
    Manuel.   It is a cause where swords play little part.
    Dolores.   Please tell me who she is?   Now do.
    Manuel.   I shall,
Provided that you try to guess her name.
    Dolores.   I am the poorest guesser in the world.
    Manuel.   Dolores—
    Dolores.   Ah—what—did you—say to me?
    Manuel.   I only got that far.
    Dolores.   What was the rest?
    Manuel.   I really think there is no more to say.
    Dolores.   That was an exclamation of no sense.
    Manuel.   It meant so much to me.
    Dolores.   How so?
    Manuel.   • Because
It answered what you asked.
    Dolores.   Now what was that?
    Manuel.   Who is the one I love—then if you'd know—
Dolores, it is you, you are my love
Come, let us lay aside this pretty farce,
And tell me truly, is my love returned?
    Dolores.   And you have loved me for—wait, let me
         see—
There 's one, two, three, yes, nearly four short months;
The time is brief to learn so deep a thing.
    Manuel.   Although despotic circumstance enticed
From me two years of sweet acquaintanceship,
I did not have to learn to love at all
So quickly did your presence make me slave:
But I have lived in those four doubtful months
As many weary years, except the hours

When you were by, and they were always short;
Like sweetest things in life they lingered not.
    Dolores. How rapidly your years must hurry on,
I would not see you age at such a pace,
For fear your youthful days would be confined
To far too brief a period; for youth
Is short enough; when it is gone, fades love;
That love which nature grants alone to youth.
    Manuel. O, then regard my love, and save my youth,
That it may taste the sweets denied in age;
I loved you from the day that we first met,
So let me have the shadow of reward.
    Dolores. The shadow, Manuel, 's too light a thing—
But—if reality will compensate—
I hardly think it may—I—
    Manuel.   Then you do?
O where 's the hour that can this time surpass?
All happiness that 's past, was pain till now:
I win and yet you did not tell me how.
    Dolores. You knew too well, dear Manuel, the art.

*Enter Gov. Fages and Don Pablo unseen by stage. Don
    Pablo is surprised. Gov. Fages extends his hand.
    Don Pablo grasps it, and gestures silence.*

    Don Pablo. Let them enjoy their secret, it is dear;
This time will be so hallowed in their lives.
    Gov. Fages. It shall be so. *Aside.* Well, this looks
        like success:
Here is a day wherein I 've lost and won.
    To Don Pablo. The union of fond hearts do not delay.
    Don Pablo. No more than courtship 's dear necessity.

Their lives now joined, shall never drift apart;
For Love 's transfixed them with his magic dart.

Exeunt Gov. Fages and Don Pablo.

SCENE II.—Interior of Father Serra's Home at San Carlos. Afternoon, August 28, 1784.

Enter Fathers Serra and Palou.

Father Serra. I 'm very glad that you arrived in time:
The summons that I sent with my farewell
To have a Father from the Missions near
Take leave in person, will be most too late.
Father Palou. I hoped that Father Sitjar would arrive.
Father Serra. He will not be in time. I would have liked
To also see dear Father Pieras,
But then the Mission would be left alone.
Your being here recalls old times again:

How sorrowful seemed dedication day,
When Santa Clara was, with holy rites,
Forever consecrated to the Faith,
To know that Father Murguía lay
Beneath the Church he labored so to build:
Poor Father Peña must be lonesome now.

Father Palou.   The sad condition I 'll encounter soon.
Father Serra.   Ah, yes; for one of the three friends
remain.
Father Palou.   You 'll never know my feelings now.
Alone.
Father Serra.   I know that feeling well.   But two
short years
And little more since Father Crespi died.
Father Palou.   He was the life and sunshine of our lives.
Father Serra.

What sorrow, what bereavement, comes with death;
To look for the last time on one we love,
And know that nevermore the passing breath
Will animate the form whose soul 's above.
It 's then, I feel the world is lost to me,
That I must wander lonely through this life,
Before me no bright future can I see,
A dark existence only, filled with strife.
Most in this life must pass through such an hour,
Some sink beneath the strain to not survive,
One must be aided by a stronger power
To stay the bitter shocks Death will contrive.
Outlive the time, in time to come, we may;
But in this life I know no sadder day.

Father Palou. O, He who calls thee home, would summon me.

Father Serra. We must abide His pleasure, dearest friend.
I did not hope to leave San Gabriel,
And Father Sanchez thought I 'd not survive·
And loved Cruzado then proposed to have
The Sacramental rites administered;
When all at once I felt I would be spared;
But now I feel that He is calling me.
Give my farewell to your associate,
Dear Father Cambon, whom I will see no more.

Father Palou. I shall.

Father Serra.   Francisco, I am not content.

Father Palou. Vie with the world no more. Be tranquil now.

Father Serra. My life has been so short, your Reverence;
It seems to me but little while ago
I was in manhood's prime, and farther back,
My memory is good, I was a youth
For whom a most attractive future lay:
My thoughts now backward turn to conquests past
And from the verge of faculties' decay,
I see the spirit of my early dreams
Accomplished in the line of Christian work:
But still I wished to save more gentile souls
Than I had done, and now it is too late;
A voice within me says, "Renounce your toil
For your allotted time to save, is past,"—
It is indeed,—conversion days are o'er,

And lamentations will avail me not:
Now comes that long-expected final hour
When nearer with its dark approach the bier
Appears in its sepulchral fantasy;
And through the mist of mystery my soul
Will take its flight to seek the life renewed;
So dies the form and back to dust returns,
So lives the spirit in eternal peace.

    Father Palou. Would all of us could do what you
        have done.
Have no regrets; your life 's an answered prayer.

    Father Serra. It 's now long past the time when we
        should hear
Of the petitions and complaints I sent;
The franking privilege, the Mission guards,
And escorts for the friars on their trips,
The founding of new Missions down the coast,
The need of posts in the interior,
The governor's contempt at our requests,
The use of runaways to work for him,
And other things I wrote about last March
And months before: have they forgotten us?

    Father Palou. The time is long but then official acts
Are so encumbered by formalities:
The viceroy is a just and pious man;
Trust him, your Reverence.

    Father Serra.   All may be well. *Exeunt.*

    Enter Father Noriega and Eduardo.

    Father Noriega. When does Captain Cañizares re-
turn to Monterey?

Eduardo. He has departed, Father.

Father Noriega. It is to be regretted that Governor Fages and family are absent in San Francisco: our Father Presidente is sinking rapidly: although he 's able to be up, the surgeon says he 'll not survive the day.

Eduardo. I am thankful he received the last Sacrament.

Father Noriega. Yes, and the Absolution and Plenary Indulgence of our Order.

Eduardo. Does Father Diaz of the *San Carlos* remain with us?

Father Noriega. Until the end, my son. Has Captain Soler arrived?

Eduardo. Juan told me he sent the adjutant-inspector word to come over immediately.

Father Noriega. I hope he will arrive in time. What of Captain Alvarez?

Eduardo. I sent him word. Don Pablo and family will remain throughout the day.

Enter Ignacio.

Ignacio. Father, a messenger just arrived from Mission Dolores, sent by Governor Fages. He bore this packet.

Father Noriega. Very well, Ignacio. *Exit Ignacio.* They contain orders from the viceroy and advices from the College. Strange why they were sent to the Presidio of San Francisco. I shall look them over; there may be news of interest to our president. *Exit.*

Eduardo. May I be granted just a little time to see

the Father before he dies.   I lose a friend that cannot be replaced.

Enter Fathers Serra and Palou.

Father Serra.   Yes, I will see Eduardo now.   Send him to me.   Here he is.

Exit Father Palou.

Eduardo.   My Father.

Father Serra.   Rise, my son.   Tell me, have you decided to abandon your hopes of priesthood?

Eduardo.   Your Reverence, after studying this question from every standpoint; thinking deeply over the smallest details; and of late not permitting my affections to sway me in the least; I came to this firm and irrevocable decision, that it is my duty, so long as our Heavenly Father chooses to grant me life, to devote every moment of my time to His Holy Church, for the spiritual and material advancement of my fellow-men.

Father Serra.   How grand is this resolve.   You have acted a noble part in your struggle against a strong temptation.   There is no severer test of character than to resist the mighty power of the affections. My wish shall be fulfilled.   Have you heard from Manuel or Dolores?

Eduardo.   No, Father, I avoided meeting them since I made my peace with Manuel, the day after our quarrel.   I felt it was wisest to shun those influences which might tend to affect my decision.

Enter Ignacio.

Father Serra.   *Aside.*   Wisdom as well as enthusiasm. Ignacio?

Ignacio. Captain Alvarez has arrived, Father.

Father Serra. Most opportune! I should like to see the captain here.

Exit Ignacio. Enter Manuel.

Manuel. I heard that you were failing, Father; I hope it is not true. I 'm glad to see you, Eduardo.

Father Serra. I fear it is, my son. Have you any news for me?

Manuel. Nothing, Father,—except—well—I heard that you were worse and came—

Father Serra. Yes, I know; and you were kind to think of this old man. But I should like to have that little news.

Manuel. I 'm afraid it will offend—

Eduardo. Manuel, whatever you may say will give me no offense.

Father Serra. That is the right spirit, my son.

Manuel. I have been engaged to Señorita Dolores for some time and it is Don Pablo's wish the bans be announced the first Sunday of November.

Father Serra. Manuel, it is good news! It is happy news! I learned it from Señor Valencia; but I wanted Eduardo to know it from your lips. Would that I could live to make announcement. A dying Father's blessing for you both.

Eduardo. Manuel, accept my sincere congratulations. You were right; I was wrong.

Manuel. Eduardo, I felt I was advising what was right. Had you married Dolores I would still say you erred.

When I told you she loved me I had had flashes of encouragement.   And, Father, I now see Don Pedro is
wrong in many of his rulings on Mission affairs, and as
my office in Monterey has been made permanent, I will
do as I promised Eduardo on my return last March, that
is induce the governor to be more lenient; more con-
siderate; more just.

Father Serra.   At last my hopes of you are realized.
The governor has injured us, but I am soon to pass
away, and he no doubt will rule for many years—so,
Manuel, tell him I send a last forgiveness for his opposition and will pray as I often have before that he will
become a wiser man.

Manuel.   He cannot but think kindly on hearing
your message.

Father Serra.   Manuel, Eduardo can rejoice with you,
for he has wisely decided that a holy life is best.

Eduardo.   Yes, I know my life-work now.   She will
be happy, and I am satisfied.

Father Serra.   My children, you have made glad the
heart of a dying man.   Kneel and receive my blessing.
Now, Manuel, tell Father Palou I wish to see him; and
Eduardo, request Father Noriega's presence here.

Exeunt Eduardo and Manuel.

So ends the struggle, happily for all.

Enter Fathers Palou and Noriega.

Fathers, I wish to speak with you.   Eduardo.   Did he
return?

Father Palou.   I will call him.   *Exit.*

Father Noriega. I hope you are feeling no worse?

Father Serra. I am a little stronger than I was an hour ago.

Enter Father Palou and Eduardo.

Let me commend to your love and care a youth who has won a mighty victory in following the dictates of duty, not desire; he is destined to make a most enthusiastic worker for the Church; Fathers, think well of my young protege, he is faithful. Give him letters to our Guardian and to our friend, Archbishop Haro, and also to Padre Fermin Lausen, stating it was one of my last requests that he be aided in every way, for he was under my care, and promises most well.

Father Palou. Eduardo merits praise, he always did; I will do for him most gladly all you wish.

Father Noriega. He shall ever have my love and care.

Eduardo. Your Reverences, I humbly thank you.

Father Serra. Let me go and bless the neophytes. Assist me, Eduardo. *Exeunt.*

Father Palou. How much I wish some news would come to brighten his last hours.

Father Noriega. That blessing has been granted him.

Father Palou. What!

Father Noriega. The long expected news from Mexico has arrived.

Father Palou. Possible! Favorable?

Father Noriega. No message could much greater blessings bring.

Father Palou. The hand of God.

Father Noriega. But perhaps the news might be dangerous to impart; he 's very weak.

Father Palou. His weakness is a kind that will gather strength on favorable reports. By all means let him know of it.

Enter Father Serra and Eduardo.

Father Serra. My friends, I have a marvel to relate;
Last night I had a strange experience,—
It evidenced a holy man's reward.
As I was kneeling in a fervent prayer,
A sudden blank occurred, then I awoke
To find myself upon the desert waste;
I knew the place from many old reports;
For weird, and dark, and silent at my feet,
The Rio Colorado flowed along;
I stood upon a little rocky knoll
And round about there seemed the evidence
Of pre-historic man.   The night was such
I could not see with clearness far away,
More than define the ghostly sentinels,
The cacti, yucca, and agava tall:
Then all at once the place became illumed,
The moonlight shone across the cactus plain
And burst upon my view quite near to me,
The blackened ruins of a massacre.
It was Concepcion.   All was so still—
When suddenly to westward and afar,
A hidden choir sang out in ecstasy
The strains we 're wont to sing upon a death;
A fallen cause seemed glorified in it;

And with the song three mournful bells intoned
Their saddened chimes; how strange my feelings were:
Now comes the vision's most absorbing scene;
So sad, so beautiful: for there appeared
From out a bank of sombre western clouds,
A phantom host that toward the ruins came;
They were the souls of the uncoffined dead;
The incense-bearers led the spectral front,
Then came the holy martyrs, four in all;
Upon their sacred brows the nimbus shone,
And o'er their faces was the light of joy:
Oh! God, forgive the sin, I envied them.
Then near appeared I thought a penitent,
It was the figure of a Yuma chief
That gazed with horror on the sacred line;
The Padres turned, and sadly looked at him,
On which he cried in tones so terrified,
" Look not at me in that reproachful way,
For I am not the author of your woes."
With one accord they blessed him and passed on,
Then twice around the blasted ruins marched
And through the charred remains from north to south,
Then east to west, they made the Holy Cross;
Upon completing which, the music ceased;
The clouds that banked the east shone with a light
Unlike that which I 'd ever seen before;
The grandest chorus then, I ever heard,
With ' Tantum Ergo' made the Heavens ring;
Then countless angels on the scene appeared
And lined an open way before the place
Whence came the wondrous light that covered all;

That center point my eyes could not define,
So like the sun it seemed: the martyrs rose
And through the open space they made their way,
And followed those who followed them on earth;
To those bright regions where the faithful go,
The place where pain and sorrow is unknown.
The mighty angel chorus fainter grew,
And as their voices died away, the light
Failed rapidly, and mist o'ercame the scene,
In which the vision merged and then was lost:
And at the end bowed I my head in prayer,
And gave my thanks that God should let me see
This grand reception to the dead rehearsed;
For nature's great cathedral never held
A vision quite so wondrous beautiful.

    Father Noriega. Oh! this is marvelous!

    Father Palou.   It 's wonderful! ·

    Eduardo. What an experience!

    Father Noriega.   Blest be their names!

    Father Palou. I can commit your sin, and envy too.

    Father Noriega. I wish I could have been with you
        last night.

    Eduardo. Thanks be to God, that I have chosen right.

    Father Serra. You have, my son: how stable was the
        proof.

My friends, I wish you all had been with me.

    Father Palou. O, Mother Church, what touching
        miracles,

Thy all embracing Faith presents to man.

    Eduardo. How would your Reverence interpret it—
The vision of the souls?

 Father Serra.   I 'll tell you how:
I took it as a great presentiment
Of my approaching end, it seemed to me
Like a reward for what I had endured.

 Father Palou. Aside. How well thy life deserves a
  like return.
 Father Serra. And from it did I draw the promise that
The blessed land, our California,
Would rise in triumph o'er its enemies
As did the Fathers to immortal life.
 Father Noriega. Indeed! Indeed! how plainly is it
  shown.

Father Palou.   No deed of state shall keep this land
    obscure!
When I explored the great peninsula
I was impressed with the surrounding views.
Across a wide expanse of sandy dunes
My way led to the stretch of ocean beach,
And going north I climbed the rocky cliffs;
Across the strait and on the northern shore,
Bold headlands reared their summits 'bove the sea,
Between the rugged shores, the rising tide
Came flowing in, and all along the coast
The barking cries of countless noisy seals
Made with the gulls an animated scene:
'T was then I felt this hidden western bay
Was fated, as the time rolled on, to hold
Much of the trade sent out from distant lands,
And make the port one of much prominence.
    Father Serra.   Ah! Fathers, I as well have been im-
    pressed;
For ever since the day I first said Mass
At Monterey, beneath the mighty oak,
Within whose trunk we drove the nail to hang
The holy crucifix, until to-day;
Aye, even from the time when first we gazed
From off Espiritu Santo and saw
Spread out the land-locked San Diego bay,—
An interval of over fifteen years,—
I never ceased to feel the deepest love
For California; she has my prayers.
But, Father, it is not alone the port;
Before me now a golden era looms;

Progressive spirits will invade these wilds,
And coming, stay; there are attractions here:
Within these mountain borders are contained
All things that needy man can ever want,
For Nature reveled in her lavishment
And left a masterpiece terrestrial:
If ever distant shores were to be known,
And in the knowing, recognized as great;
Then o'er the name of California,
Entwine the seal and symbols of success!

Father Noriega. A prophecy the world will see fulfilled.

Father Palou. It will be so.

Father Noriega. I have received our official mail from Mexico. It was enclosed with the governor's packet and in consequence forwarded to San Francisco. It just arrived from there.

Father Palou. It is the news you waited for so long.

Father Serra. At last! Are the orders favorable to us?

Father Noriega. So much so that your faith in California will be doubly strengthened.

Father Serra. I wish few sweeter joys.

Father Palou. Is the president's license to confirm, renewed?

Father Noriega. Reads document. It is to be.

Father Serra. My successor shall have the privilege.

Father Noriega. This is welcome;—the governor is warned to moderate his actions toward the friars or he will lose his position and honors.

Father Serra. A timely reprimand.

Father Palou. Does this information come direct from the viceroy?

Father Noriega.   No, but he instructed the College to inform us privately of these orders.

Father Serra.   We have friends in Mexico.

Father Palou.   San Fernando looks well to the interest of its missionaries.

Father Serra.   Are there any more?

Father Noriega.   The governor is ordered to return all fugitive neophytes to the Missions, and not use them for labor at the Presidios.

Father Serra.   Our complaints regarding them were not to pass unheeded.

Father Noriega.   He is also ordered to give all the necessary aid requested, to bring the fugitives back from the rancherias.

Father Serra.   This is excellent news.

Father Palou.   But we had long to wait for it.

Father Serra.   When is the governor expected back from San Francisco?

Eduardo.   He sends word he will remain this month. The Señora is ill at Mission Dolores.

Father Palou.   He can have time to reflect upon the wisdom of his orders before returning to Monterey.

Father Serra.   What of mission guards? mentioned?

Father Noriega.   Yes, they are to be increased to a sufficiency; and hereafter when the friars journey they are to have the adequate protection requested.

Father Serra.   How glorious is the news! I am impatient to hear it all. What of the franking privilege?

Father Noriega.   The *Junta* has ordered the governor not to enforce the obnoxious law.

Father Palou. A wise command. December last, your Reverence wrote of that.

Father Serra. And twice since then. Nine months we 've had to wait.

Father Palou. What of new friars?

Father Noriega. The Guardian is arranging to send new missionaries immediately.

Father Serra. A long felt want to be a need no more!

Father Palou. Excellent!

Father Serra. There must be more!

Father Palou. Tell all!

Father Noriega. What I will now read outweighs all previously declared.

Father Serra. About new missions, I am sure!

Father Noriega. It touches that.

Father Palou. When comes success, misfortune tarries not!

Father Serra. A flood of glad tidings!

Father Noriega. Supplies and men for the founding of the proposed Missions of Santa Barbara and La Purísima Concepcion are to be immediately collected, foundings made, and building commenced.

Father Serra. At last, at last! after all these years! How good is God to comfort one so humble as am I.

Father Palou. The best, the most interesting of all!

Father Noriega. A greater follows.

Father Serra. More!

Father Palou. Impossible!

Father Serra. Is this a dream?

Father Noriega. A sweet reality. The intended line of Missions to extend in the interior from north to south, that our Father-Presidente outlined, now seems a near possibility. The Council of the Indes orders they be considered, and expeditions sent to explore the territory.

Father Serra. Glorious news to a failing man! Now can I pass away somewhat recompensed.

Father Palou. It is grand!

Father Serra. Wonderful!

Eduardo. And secularization receives a blow!

Father Noriega. Indeed it does.

Father Palou. Our prayers are answered.

Father Serra. This news though long delayed with
           greeting 's hailed,
To date nine Missions have been founded, yet
That number falls far short of what we planned;
I will not live to see another reared
For all there 's left to me is prayer and death;
But prayers I 'll offer now, and after that,
To have our Christian objects entertained.
Push on with haste the new stone church that is
To take the place of this adobe one;
Complete the works I have projected here:
Extend the confirmations everywhere!
O, friars, labor as Saint Francis did
For souls that trust to heresies for hope:
Can wild environments hold forth to them
The hope of resurrection after death?
No, for they need the guidance of the priests
To take them kindly by the hand and say,
'My children, let the Fathers guide you to
The universal and accepted Church.'

Father Palou. The Faith our Fathers held so sacredly.

Father Noriega. God made the Church, it 's indefecti-
ble.

Eduardo. Man made the State which is the prey of
time.

Father Serra. Ah, son, that brings to mind our
enemy.
Let not the State in mocking sorrow sing
A requiem o'er ruins of the Church,
Nor when officials smile think they are friends
And turn to plots an inattentive ear:
They 'll try all means to break the Fathers' rule,
Forbear to interfere when they may act
Will usher in the epoch of our fall.
But friends, while they may wreck the Missions here,
The principles of creed they cannot touch;
For though our blessed Faith is constantly
Assailed by argument, assailed by foe,
The Cross in triumph ever will emerge!
Catholicism has reigned for ages now,
The master creed of races and of climes;
It will continue past the time these walls
Become the dust of which they were composed,
And when our memories are lost like those
Innumerable ones, who 've passed away
Recorded not by legend, line or stone.

Falls back exhausted in Eduardo's arms.

Eduardo. Our Father 's dying!
Father Serra. No.
Father Noriega. Rest, Father, rest.
Father Palou. Be seated here, dear friend.

Father Noriega.   .   Are you
  in pain?

Father Serra.   Exhausted, only; I am free from pain.

Eduardo. Aside.   So noble in the highest sentiments.
No poet's pen in elegy sublime
Your life can picture, or your deeds relate,
And justly give you due.

Father Serra.   I 'm better now.

Father Noriega.   These charges shall be strictly followed out.

Father Palou.   We 'll watch the old regime with
  greatest care.

Father Serra.   What is that crying sound? the neo-
  phytes?
Are they so quickly sorrowed on reports?
Go, Father, and Eduardo, comfort them.

Father Noriega. Aside.   They have a cause to weep;
  they 're losing you.

  Exeunt Father Noriega and Eduardo.

Father Serra.   Francisco, when I 'm summoned and
  shall stand
In presence of the Holy Trinity,
I 'll pray for you, for California,
And with my lowly prayers I 'll supplicate
Saint Joseph, aye, and our Saint Francis too,
That they may help our Order in its trials.

Father Palou.   May great success attend you, dearest
  friend.
Ah, no, you could not other than succeed.

Father Serra.   I do not feel as confident as you;

My sins may yet debar acknowledgement
That I deserve to thus be recognized.
The carpenter has made my coffin? no?

   Father Palou. ' T was finished, Father, late last even-
      ing.

   Father Serra. It 's well. Francisco, you have labored
      long;
You should retire.

   Father Palou. I think I shall depart
The coming year; for long I 've wished to write
A record of your ceaseless toiling life.

   Father Serra. To write my life account would honor
      me
Much more than I deserve. My place is low,
My name 's unknown except to very few.

   Father Palou. O pardon me, our country knows you
      well.
I beg you let me take that comfort kind,
As rest to my old age, and write your life.

   Father Serra. Then in my history do not omit
My many faults, nor should you as my friend,
Invest my sins with cloak of lenience.

   Father Palou. I 'll aim to be a just biographer.
Aside. How can I write the faults of faultless men?
There 'll be pathetic music in those lines
That tell the virtue of his services.
Here 's one of whom posterity will say,
'He was the greatest man that ever trod
The sands of Alta California.'

   Father Serra. Now, Father, will you grant my last
      request?

Father Palou.   Beloved President, what e'er you ask.
Father Serra.   Then bury me beside the one we
      loved,
Dear Father Crespi, in the Mission Church,
Amid the scenes so many years our home:
Although it seems a wrong requesting that
I rest so near to one who never sinned,
Yet the vicinity is sanctified,
And resting there may purify a soul
That had in life a need of constant prayer.
Father Palou.   That disposition 's one we settled on,
Your Reverence.
Father Serra.   I thank you for intents.
Was that a moan?
Father Palou.   The neophytes again
Voice out their sorrows over your decline.
Father Serra.   Go speak to them, the faithful In-
      dians:
But let me have a glass of water first.
Father Palou.   Eduardo, there?

Enter Eduardo.

Eduardo.   What is the Father's
      will?
Father Palou.   A glass of water for his Reverence.

Exit Eduardo.

Father Serra.   Was that Eduardo?
Father Palou.   Yes.

Father Serra.   Have him
come in.

Enter Eduardo with water.

Father Serra. Bless you for that.   You should not
    seem so sad.
Eduardo. I know—I cannot help—O Infinite!
Do spare the good kind friend of these past years.
Father Serra. There, there, Eduardo; do not weep for
    me;
A man is he that can a grief forget:
I 'm happy now, for soon I shall be there;
Then I will meet the Padres of the past,
And see the greatest of departed ones.
Now go with my dear friend and tell them why,
The neophytes, they should not mourn for me;
And I will rest alone a little while.
Father Palou. But, Father, shall we leave—
Father Serra.   He 's
    ever near.

Exeunt Father Palou and Eduardo.

*Father Serra goes to the door, looks out on the face of Nature,
seems troubled a moment, then his countenance becomes calm.
He returns and reclines on a couch.*

Enter Father Palou.

Goes slowly to where Father Serra is lying, bends over him, starts, breathes a silent prayer to heaven.

Father Palou.   Eduardo.

Enter Eduardo.

The bells.

Exit Eduardo.   The bells toll.

FINIS.

EPILOGUE.

While Padre Serra's part long since was played,
His sepulcher is yet uncarved and rough;
Therein by friends in simple sorrow laid,
Though honored some he 's honored not enough.
In ruined state his Missions stand to-day,
A sad reproach to Time's progressive hand;
A mournful commentary on the way,
The great are left forgotten by their land:
And in my thoughts of him this came to me
When thinking of the grave wherein he lies;
As none earned sculptured marble more than he,
Here is a noble soul to canonize.

    One now can say, though he to fame was born,
    Here lies a man, great honors left forlorn.